DRINKWATER

By

Otto Scamfer

DRINKWATER

By

Otto Scamfer

First Printing 2008
By
Custom Books Publishing

Copyright © 1993 By Otto Scamfer

*To all of those who struggle in the battle against alcoholism—
never give up the fight!*

TABLE OF CONTENTS

CHAPTER ONE

As usual, I was drunk and in trouble, but this time I was in serious trouble. I found myself in a predicament where I could be dead within minutes.

"We know you're here!" A man shouted. "Come out and show yourself!" I didn't answer him, though I recognized the voice. It was my father's bailiff, Cyrus Everett.

Being in no condition to fight, I set my eyes upon the forest around me for a better place to hide. The landscape was dotted with enormous oaks and towering pines, but none of them appeared to offer any greater refuge than the immense oak I was already standing behind. For the moment, I decided to stay where I was.

While hiding behind the huge tree, my body trembled and I noticed a thin gray fog settling in over the woodland. Suddenly, from the corner of my eye, a movement caught my attention and I turned to see what had caused it. I was relieved to find that it was only an oak leaf falling from its branch peacefully toward the ground.

Silence reigned for the next few moments except for the sound of my own breath. I listened intently for any other noise my ears could detect—nothing. My pursuers must be quietly lurking about, I reasoned, but exactly where and how many of them there were, I did not know.

The silence overwhelmed me and my thoughts became broken and meandering. A memory of being a young lad in the same forest where I now stood began clouding my mind. I saw myself as a child playing with my friend Eric. We were pretending to be knights in the king's army and we attacked each other with sticks as our weapons. As we frolicked, a kind old hermit who we had often seen in the woods came near. He greeted us cheerfully and—

"There he is!" shouted an unfamiliar voice. "We've got him now!"

The ale in my blood had let my mind wander causing my body to relax. This, in turn, had caused the end of my sword, still in its scabbard, to stick out from behind the tree where I was hiding. My pursuers had spotted it and now they knew exactly where I was.

My mind stumbled as it realized again the situation I was in. With my eyes peering out from behind the great oak, I saw only two men. I decided to face them.

Cyrus Everett was a bulky man with a broad head. His eyes were bantam compared to the puffy cheeks and spacious forehead that surrounded them. Between those two black dots projected a round pudgy nose. His chin, which was sunken back towards his neck, was wide and had a day's growth of beard on it. He was bald except for a sparse bit of black and gray that encircled the back and sides of his heavy skull. As he climbed down from his horse, I was able to view his enormous pear-shaped body that bulged at the seams of his dusky wool jacket.

Though I had seen this man a thousand times before, it was then that I realized just how ugly he was. Throughout my life I had never befriended him, for he was not a friendly man. Somehow though, I had managed to get along with him. After all, he was my father's friend and bailiff and he was trusted with everything my father owned. That was, of course, until now.

The other man, who was already off of his horse and walking toward me, I had not seen before or at least I didn't recognize. He was tall with lengthy stray wisps of hair that fluttered in front of his dark brown eyes. He had a sharp narrow nose that jutted outward above his broad lips—lips that curled into a wry grin as I gazed upon him.

Stepping out from behind the tree, I yelled. "Cyrus, before we fight, I must know one thing!"

"What is it my boy?" he asked with a fiendish grin.

"Why did you kill my father?"

"Kill your father? Ha! I didn't kill your father! It was you who took his life! By drinking and fighting and lying to him, it was you, Winston Taber, who killed him!"

"Say what you want, Cyrus! I won't believe your treacherous lies!"

"Then answer this! How many noble sons have ever been sent home from their training as a knight? How many can you name? I can think of only one—you Winston! Only you!"

My mind was growing numb. It was hard enough to think in such a desperate situation and still worse with the ale clouding my head. Cyrus' accusations confused me even more, for it was true, I had recently been sent home from Baron Simon's castle. I had been learning the ways of a knight, but the drink was beginning to destroy me and I was sent home in disgrace. Even so, my father had still loved me and that was probably his downfall. The important men in our village thought he was weak for not banishing me from his home and Cyrus had obviously taken note of the situation.

"Ah! So I've touched a nerve, have I? Why don't you speak? You drunkard!"

"Shut up! I'm no drunkard! You're the one who murdered my father! The proof is that you've come to kill me too!"

"You're brighter than I thought young lad," replied Cyrus smiling like a serpent, "and I owe you the service of telling you the truth before I kill you. It was I who did such a tragic deed to your father, but no one else knows and no one else shall find out!"

"But what of your friend here?" I slurred. "Now he knows!"

Cyrus gave a quick ill glance at his companion and this disturbed the tall wiry man immensely as was told by the expression on his face. The slim man's smile was rapidly displaced by an awkward frown, but Cyrus was fast and said, "Hector is my friend and he trusts in me as I trust in him. He would never tell a soul about what I've said here. He shall gain in the spoils of my plan!"

The tall man, Hector, quickly replaced his frown with a smirk and he took a step toward me with self-assurance.

"Then tell me this! How will you explain my death to the village officials and to my mother?"

"That," replied Cyrus, "has already been taken care of. After killing your father, I told everyone at the castle how I found him lying in a pool of his own blood. I said that in his last breaths of life he told me that it was you, his only son, drunk as you are now, who stabbed him in a fit of rage!" Cyrus paused for a moment and chuckled jubilantly.

I stared at his fat flushing face and realized that the man's arrogance was beyond comprehension. Cyrus was proud of the fiendish crime he had committed and he spoke as though he wanted me to congratulate him on a plan well carried out.

"Once I've taken care of you," he continued, "I'll merely tell the county steward that you resisted arrest and that I took your life in self-defense. Now let's stop this chatter and get on with it!"

Enraged by the words Cyrus had spoken, I pulled my sword from its scabbard, stumbling slightly in my drunkenness. Unfortunately, I hadn't had the chance to grab my shield in my hasty departure from the village. Now I faced two men with shields and swords without any protection of my own.

Cyrus laughed while Hector stepped back knowing that he would only be needed if the fat man got into trouble.

Cyrus was a capable swordsman though he wasn't a knight. He had much experience with the use of a sword in his duties as a bailiff. I, on the other hand, was but an armiger who had just recently received my sword in ceremony before being sent home from Baron Simon's manor. My only chance was to strike first and pray for God's protection.

Before I could attack, Cyrus lunged at me with a loud grunt. Luckily, being a heavy man, he was not terribly quick. While still feeling the effects of ale, I was able to dodge the blow and at the same time I tried a cut to his left side. My sword thudded against his shield and Cyrus roared with laughter.

"You clumsy ox! Did you hope to get the best of me? You won't find me as easy a foe as the young lads you played with in your childhood!"

"No!" I screamed, rage coursing through my body. "You shall be easier to slaughter than the overfed pigs which are served on the king's table!" I leaped at him and lunged my sword at his enormous belly, any second expecting to feel my sword cut into his soft flesh.

Instead, I felt the piercing pain of a blade slicing into my left shoulder as my sword again fell harmlessly upon his shield. I smelled the pungent odor of my own blood and my mind grew hazy. As the red fluid drained from my shoulder, so did my confidence and my rage was replaced with fear.

"Is it a fool, or a drunk, or the two combined, who lets his own anger get the best of him?" Cyrus asked, but I gave him no reply, for I was pondering whether to run or continue fighting.

Then swiftly, Cyrus brought his sword down upon me. I dodged and was able to block the strike with my blade, but he lunged again and again in a frenzy. Each time I took a step back while trying to block and dodge every blow. He drew blood from my chest several times though fortunately the wounds were minor.

It seemed like hours went by as he charged and I retreated. At one point, I looked abreast to see the wide lips of Hector pinched up in a grin. He was enjoying what he saw. This, through my anger, gave me strength for a moment. I wildly hacked and charged and swung my sword at Cyrus. His face paled and changed from that of a man winning a game to that of someone who was actually in a battle for his life. He stumbled backward over a fallen tree limb and I placed a good jab, though not deep, into his gut. His pudgy face winced with pain, but my triumph lasted only a moment and the plump fleshy man again began to return blows with his sword. Once more I found myself retreating.

Then suddenly I saw it. I knew nothing of how it got there, no memory of the thrust or jab, I just saw it was there and I knew in a second I would feel its pain. Cyrus' blade stuck into the left center of my chest and I was sure it pierced my heart. From the satisfied appearance on the corpulent man's face, he too was confident of the lethality of my injury. Then came the pain, rushing from my wound like the ripples made from a stone thrown into a smooth pond. With each wave the pain grew stronger and so did the realization of death. Cyrus spat and withdrew his sword.

I collapsed on the carpet of leaves that covered the forest's floor. Was this to be my end? I wondered. Could this be all my life would lead too? A lonely death? Drunk and afraid?

"How does it feel to be at death's door? Not so good huh? You should have listened to your tutors more closely and stayed away from so much drink! You may not believe so, but it was you who brought this all about, not I! And I will not feel guilty for a moment, not over the death of a drunkard!" Cyrus stopped and sucked in some air for a moment before continuing. "May you have enough time to make peace with God before you take your last breath!" The heavy man turned and walked away.

Awash with pain and fear, Cyrus Everett's words rang in my ears. Could it really have been me, by drinking and fighting, which had caused my father to lose control over his diminutive domain? Was I the cause of his death in a roundabout way? Maybe.

The wound in my chest was excruciating. Blood was oozing from it, but not like it should have had it been truly a mortal wound. I laid still and shut my eyes, not wanting Cyrus to think I was still alive. I was sure he thought his blade had cut into my heart and that I was already dead.

"Argh!" I surprisingly heard and I opened my eyes while keeping my head still. Through the branches and leaves obstructing part of my view, I could see why Hector was screaming. Out of the front of his tall quivering body shone the long red blade of a sword and behind him stood Cyrus with a firm grip on the hilt. The fat man, with his husky right leg, kicked Hector forward while pulling out his blade.

Hector's knees buckled under him and he fell face first onto the hard ground. His body shook violently for a moment and then became still.

"Fool! You didn't deserve to live if you were so stupid as to believe I would trust you!" Cyrus barked and then spat on the ground. He cursed and grumbled as he strode toward his horse. Then after grabbing the reins of Hector's steed and mounting his own, he took one more glance at me. I made sure not to breathe. He seemed satisfied that I was dead and he rode off into the mist of the forest.

I laid there in the woodland and listened to the fading sound of the horse's hoofs. Quietness soon enveloped the grove and I tried to sit up but the pain was unbearable. I inspected the cut on my left shoulder and saw that it had stopped bleeding. The extensive wound on my chest still trickled blood and a pool of crimson had formed on the earth beside me. I moved my right hand to my backside and I could feel a flow of blood where Cyrus' blade had exited.

I must make it to the village and tell someone what happened, I reasoned. Again I tried to sit up and, ignoring the pain, I succeeded. Then, with all my strength, I stood. A sharp piercing pang shot through my chest, but I gritted my teeth and took a step toward Hector's lifeless body. At the same time, I felt something tickling the back of my throat. I coughed to relieve the discomfort and spat. My spit was bright red and when I saw this, the realization of my own mortality came over me and I collapsed in horror.

"Please God, please don't let me die!" I cried while rolling onto my back to face the sky above me.

Gazing upward toward the heavens, I noticed a raven land on a branch of an old oak tree. Without a sound it rocked its head back and forth and glared at me with its massive black eyes. Then the earth began to spin and my vision grew dark.

*   *   *

I awoke and the sky was murky except for a white glow from the moon high above behind the cheerless clouds. The grove of trees around me was deathly still. From the light of the moon I saw a mist floating softly above the ground, its tiny wisps stretching and bending here and there like fingers. The stillness of the forest began to pound in my head like a drum. I shivered uncontrollably from the cold and my left shoulder and chest felt like they'd been stung by a thousand bees.

"Father," I prayed aloud. "I ask you now for your forgiveness and I pray that you will take me into your kingdom. Whatever you have in store for me I shall accept—be it life or death—I am ready."

Rain began to fall and it quickly turned into a heavy shower. As the water trickled down my face I moved my head and tried to inspect my wounds as best I could in the dim glow of the moonlight. My injuries no longer bled and a crust was beginning to form over the top of them. I felt around with my right hand to the wound on my back and it was hard and crusted over too.

I cleared my throat, coughed and spat. I could see that the phlegm from the back of my throat was full of blood, but its color was brown, not bright red. From what I could tell, I was no longer losing blood. To me that was a good sign despite the beliefs of the peasants and serfs who thought that bloodletting was the best thing for a sick or injured man. Instead, I believed what Shelby, my father's house servant and my tutor, had taught me. He had explained that blood was a magical fluid that kept God's spirit of life in it. It needed to flow through a man to keep him alive and if it stopped, his spirit would pass on from this world.

God's spirit still flowed through my body. I opened my mouth and let the raindrops fall upon my parched lips and dry sticky tongue. I swallowed the fresh rain and thought; never in all my days have I tasted water so sweet.

As the rain fell and pattered upon the carpet of leaves around me, my mind faded back to the events of earlier in the day.

*   *   *

That afternoon, I had been at the village brewers drinking ale and listening to the stories of the local craftsman and apprentices. Since being sent home in dishonor from my training as a knight, I had spent many such afternoons at that establishment, many more than I should have.

The sun was shining brightly for a late autumn day when I left the tavern and headed home to my father's manor. As I walked, I passed the merchants who bought and sold wines, wool, leathers, and all the wonderful things the craftsman could make. All over the village the sounds of ironworkers, stonemasons, and carpenters could be heard. I passed the bakery and smelled the delightful aroma of fresh bread as it drifted out the open windows of the cobblestone building. While crossing a lane, I tossed a few pennies to the beggars on the corner and they thanked me dearly.

"Fresh fish! Buy cheap!" shouted a peddler as I strode by his cart.

"Not today," I replied.

There were more peddlers along the way who sold coal, water, and firewood. I greeted them and they in turn greeted me. Within the high walls of the village, women and children, nobleman and peasants, knights and guildsmen went about their daily business of working, selling, and trading.

Most of the people in the village paid rent and fees or provided services, and swore an oath of loyalty to my father, Lord Tabor, or to another nobleman in a nearby town. My father bestowed his allegiance to a man of greater nobility who in turn pledged his loyalty to an even higher nobleman. This ladder of allegiance and service went all the way up to the King of England. The king himself bequeathed an oath of loyalty to God who had given him the land in return for being a wise ruler.

Soon, I was in sight of my father's manor. It was the main tower, or keep. Made of huge stones and surrounded by high walls, it stood taller and wider than any other structure in the village.

Unexpectedly, Shelby, my tutor, came running around a corner and grabbed me by the arm and pulled me into an alleyway. "Winston!" he cried. "You must hide quickly!" He pulled me back further into the alley. "Your father's dead! He's just been murdered! Everyone at the castle thinks it is you who killed him!"

"My father, dead? No, it can't be!" A wave of nausea rapidly flowed through my body as I stared into the green eyes of Shelby. "Are you sure?"

"Yes! Don't you hear me Winston? They think you killed him!"

"Ridiculous!" I shouted, anger overtaking me. My blood ran hot and I grabbed the hilt of my sword and began to pull it from its scabbard. "I shall kill the filthy pig who has done this and send him straight to hell!"

I realized then just how strong a man my tutor was. He grabbed my right arm and thrust it downward pushing my sword back into its scabbard. At the same time he caught my left arm and shoved me up against the wall. "Fool! What would you do—get yourself killed too? I told you the servants, squires, and knights of your father's castle think he died by your hands! Cyrus is rounding the men up to search for you this very minute! If you stay here you shall surely be killed!"

Finally comprehending the danger I was in, I asked, "And you? You don't believe I killed my father?"

"Winston," he replied, his long red hair tumbling about his face, "I know you better than anyone. I know you drink too much and fight too much, but I also know you would never murder your father."

"Then you must know who it is!" I exclaimed as Shelby let go of me and I stumbled forward. "Who would do such an injustice? You must know—tell me!"

"I can't be sure, but it wouldn't surprise me if Cyrus had a hand in this."

"My father's bailiff? His friend and keeper of the peace?"

"Yes, maybe, but I've no proof and he would only kill me if I accused him. I shall stay here and learn what I can, but you must go now!"

"I have no shield! I have no armor to protect me! How will I fight?"

"You won't. You'll run and hide and once you're safe you'll act like a peasant. You'll seek out your childhood friend Eric. His family will help you. Now you must go!" Shelby turned and took to his heels.

"And what of my mother? What has and shall become of her?" I called after him.

Shelby yelled back, "All I know is that she is alive and that she has been told it was you who caused this misfortune! Now go!"

With my heart pounding I stuck my head out from around the corner of the alley and peered down the lane toward the manor house. Through the open gate of the high stonewalls, I saw men running back and forth toward the entrance of my home. Then I saw the fat man, Cyrus Everett, jiggle down the narrow steps and mount his horse. He was bellowing and pointing his hands one-way and then another. The other men climbed onto their horses and with a wave of Cyrus' arm they galloped away in all directions. And I, drunk and scared, ran as fast as I could.

With my eyes on the outer walls that encircled the town, I hurried along the narrow streets toward the main gate. Soon, the stone archway of the village's entrance was above me and I faced the open fields. The wind tore at my lungs as I raced down the muddy road leading to the forest. Past the fields of cut hay, past the sheep and the cattle, past the peasants and their plows, I ran.

*   *   *

The rain had stopped and a promising glimmer of dawn was in the eastern sky. The fog from the night before was gone and the tree branches danced to a light breeze. I was chilled and my wounds ached with every beat of my heart. And my heart did beat, but how much longer? I asked myself. I was too weary and weak to get up and I doubted whether anyone would find me out in the forest. My situation appeared hopeless, but still I prayed for the chance that I might live.

And live I would! I'd quit indulging in ale and I'd cease my contentious ways! I'd live the Christian life! Oh, there was so much I could do, but so little had I done! What had I accomplished in my twenty years of life? –Drinking, fighting, and disgracing my family! And now my father was dead and everyone thought that I had killed him!

I rested there on the cold floor of the forest with hundreds of terrible thoughts and questions streaming through my mind. I was so exhausted that I couldn't grasp all their meanings or answer them clearly, but still they kept coming.

What about the love I had dreamed of sharing one day? The love you can't get from your family and friends alone. The kind of love you can only find from a women who's your best friend, whom you see only once and you know she's meant for you—someone to share every secret, every fear, and every dream. That is the kind of love I had always wanted. Now I would never know it!

I began to cry. At first just a tear, then a sob and then in the early morning breeze of a new day I began to wail. The tears streamed from my eyes like they hadn't done in years and my chest heaved and my body shook. With each wave of grief my wounds ached even more, but still I cried. There on the wet carpet of leaves I laid in a bed of anguish, hopeless and afraid, alone and dying.

Then, in a blur of tears, I saw it. A young fawn had ventured out into the grove of trees where I rested. She first rambled up to the body of Hector who laid chest down wearing a grotesque grimace on his blue-grayish face. Slowly, she wandered over to me and scratched at the earth with her hoofs. I stared into her round black eyes and she stared back at me.

What is it you want to tell me? Do you know something that I don't?

She didn't answer my thoughts, but strangely enough she came closer and licked my forehead. Her wet tongue tickled and despite my sorrows, I laughed. This startled the young fawn and she quickly dashed off into the forest. I followed her with my eyes until she disappeared, leaving me alone again.

By this time, the morning sun was rising and the woodland birds were singing their sweet songs. Being afraid that I would never wake again, I tried my best to keep sleep's gentle touch away from me. Eventually though, her delicate hands took me into their grasp. Quietly and unknowingly, I was carried off into the world of slumber.

CHAPTER TWO

I heard the faint and distant sound of rushing water and I opened my eyes. Above me was the face of a leathery old man.

"So, you're alive eh?"

I tilted my head up and gazed about me in the dim light. I was in a small cabin and a warm fire danced in the middle of the dwelling. The aroma of cabbage soup filtered through the dank musty air and suddenly I became aware that my mouth was salivating. From the flickering light, which played upon the gray barren walls, I noticed the windows had been covered with timber to block the coming winter winds. Smoke swirled leisurely about the room and made its way up toward an opening in the ceiling. The ceiling itself was made of straw that was thatched down upon a framework of wooden rafters. Around the fire, in the center of the room, was a hearth made of stone. Above the flames and upon a large tripod, whose long metal legs stretched downward to the hard stamped earth, hung a sizable kettle. In the far left corner of the cabin was a paltry table and chair. To the right was a door, which I presumed was the entrance to the structure.

An old gray terrier lay on the floor beside the bed on which I rested. When I gazed down at the hound he glanced up at me for an instant. Disinterested with what he saw, he quickly laid his furry head back down.

I crooked my head up further and strained my ears to hear the sound that had woken me.

"Ah," said the old man, "that's the stream which flows by my home. Very handy for water, and for fishing I might add."

I know this man, I thought, as I inspected his worn wrinkled face. It was thin and pale, yet it possessed strength. A fine meager nose stuck out from between two shimmering blue eyes. His hair was completely gray, what little hair he had, and matched his slim gray eyebrows. His lips were lean and when he spoke only a few white teeth jutted out from his gum line.

I tried to speak but my tongue was too dry and sticky. My throat produced only a rasping noise.

"Here," said the elderly man, handing me a horn filled with water. "Before you speak, sip this. I fetched it from the stream."

I gazed at him uneasily.

"Go on, drink it. It's clean. Besides, it's the only thing to drink around here. I've no ale or wine to offer you my noble friend."

I drank the water and then I spoke, "How do you know I'm a nobleman?"

"Ah my lad, I am old, but not stupid. What peasant or serf wears such an elegant tunic and surcoat or owns such a fine weapon, unless he has stolen them perhaps?"

"I'm not a thief!" I clamored.

The old man stood up from the stool on which he was seated and ambled over to the kettle of soup hanging above the licking flames of the fire. Grabbing a ladle, he dipped it into the steaming liquid and poured its contents into a small wooden bowl. When he was done he came over to me and held out the bowl. "Not a thief, but a murderer maybe?"

My mouth was watering terribly, so I ignored the old man's question for a moment and took the bowl. I smelled the cabbage soup and then brought it to my lips. Though it was hot, it was not too heated to prevent me from slurping down its entire contents within a few moments. When it was empty, I pulled it away from my mouth. "What do you mean, murderer?" I asked.

The old man gazed at me thoughtfully. "Yesterday," he said, "I went to Dereham to trade honey for tallow and bread. The village was astir. It seems the son of Lord Salem Tabor murdered his father in a fit of drunkenness. Luckily, the town's bailiff was able to subdue and kill the evil son, but only after the lad had killed another man by the name of Hector Vanguard. For now, the bailiff will be taking over the Lord's duties. It's quite strange though, they never found the lad's body when they went to retrieve it." For a moment the elderly man became silent and he studied my face. Then he spoke again. "I suspect this news doesn't surprise you—does it?"

I sat up quickly and placed my hand where the hilt of my sword should have been, but my blade wasn't there. Then instantly my head grew dizzy and faint. I had to lie back down on the bed.

"Don't worry," spoke the old man, "we've much time to talk. I told no one at the village about you. Now I'll get you some more medicine and then you should rest."

"Wait," I said, "where is this cabin and how did I get here?"

The aged man hesitated for a moment and then pulled up his stool to rest upon. "Two days ago, while I was foraging for mushrooms, I found you in the Staverton Forest in a grove of oaks."

"That's where I know you. You're the one I used to see in the forest when I was a little boy. I always wondered where you came from. Have you always lived out here? Why don't you live in town or just beyond the great walls near the fields with the other peasants?"

"Ah, that's another story to be told and someday maybe I'll tell it. Now hear me out. I thought you were dead when I found you. You likely should be from the wound you have in your chest." The old man's face took on a perplexing expression and he scratched at his chin for a moment. "Seems queer, that wound is where your heart should be." Then he reached out his weathered hands and put one on each side of my chest.

"What is it?" I asked.

"Well, it's just a thought, but there have been a few men throughout the ages who were born with their insides reversed."

"What do you mean? Do you mean to say my heart is on my right side?"

"Well you never know," he replied with a wink. "God's been known to do wonderful things." A moment later and with a gasp of frustration, the old man took his hands away from my chest. "I can't tell which side your heart's beating on!"

I smiled and marveled at the idea for a moment. Then I placed my hands on my chest and tried feeling for my heartbeat too, but I couldn't tell from where it was coming either. I gazed at the gray haired man. "Did you say you found me two days ago?"

"Yes, yes I did."

Two days, I thought, that's a long time to be unconscious.

The old man continued, "I managed to drag you back to my home and warm you up, but I expected you to die because disease had spread over your chest. Fortunately, I tried a remedy that was shown to me many years ago when I was in the Far East. Every day I've forced you to drink it. It works on the animals and it seems to be working on you."

"A remedy?" I questioned.

"Aye," replied the old man. Then he stood and sauntered over to a chest that rested in the corner of the one room shack. With his seasoned hands, he reached into it and pulled out a wooden box from which he took out a cloudy gray loaf of bread. Tearing off a piece of the moldy bread, he set it into a bowl. Next, the aged man poured water into the bowl and with a wooden spoon he began blending the mixture.

I couldn't believe he expected me to drink the concoction, but I also couldn't believe I was still alive. So many men are wounded in battle, I thought, but most of them die at home and in bed from disease. I gazed down at the wound on my chest. It was red, weeping, and tender to the touch. I tried to sit up again, but feeling dizzy and feverish, I had to lie back down. There was no other choice I decided, I had to drink the old man's medicine.

"Do you have a name?" I asked my elderly host.

He walked over and handed me the bowl of mush and I handed him the empty bowl of soup. "I'm Emery Fulton. Now drink up and then I'll give you some extract of willow bark to keep your fever down."

Gagging, I forced down the mixture of moldy bread and water. It tasted disgustingly like nothing I'd ever had before, but I knew it was the only thing that might possibly help me. I was in a strange and unfamiliar place, yet the old man made me feel safe and protected. I had to trust him; there was nothing else I could do.

After Emery served me two more bowls of soup and gave me the bitter extract of willow bark, I grew weary and fell asleep.

When I awoke, I glanced around the room and found the old man was gone. I sat up and surprisingly I felt neither dizzy nor feverish. I noticed too that the injury on my left shoulder was healing quite well. My chest still ached, but I felt much better than the night before. Was it last night? I wondered. I didn't know.

Just then the door of the cabin opened and Emery entered followed by his hound. "Ah, I see you're awake, just in time for breakfast too." He held up his right hand and from it hung three fat trout. "Some fish will do you good and give you strength."

"Yes," I said, nodding in agreement. "That would be pleasing." Then I laid back on the bed and watched the old man as he went about his business.

Emery set the fish on the small table in the corner of the shanty and went back outside. When he returned, he was carrying a pail of water that he placed next to the trout. Then, after pulling a knife from his soiled tunic, he began cleaning the fish with graceful movements of his worn experienced hands. First, he cut off the head of each fish and slit its gullet. Then he made two quick cuts near the throat and with his left hand he pulled out the guts. Next, after making a shallow slit along the backbone, he scooped out the bloodline with his thumb. All of this he did in a matter of seconds.

When he was done, he rinsed the trout in the bucket of water and threw them in a skillet to fry. The remains of the fish he scooped to the floor and his dog lapped them up with tail wagging pleasure.

Emery then turned to me and said, "It looks like you're feeling better and your fever has broken. Still, you'll need more medicine. I mixed some up this morning before I went fishing. Thought I'd have to pour it down your throat again like I did all day yesterday."

"All day?" I questioned.

"Aye, all day—and two days the time before. I'm getting tired of making you swallow this swill with you lying there limp as a log!"

Surprised that I had been asleep that long, I suddenly thought of my mother, Acacia. What had happened to her in the past few days? I hoped she was all right, but there was no way for me to know. Feeling frustrated, I put my hands behind my head and stared up at the ceiling. Then Emery brought me the moldy mashed up bread—what he called "medicine"—and I swallowed it in abhorrence.

A moment later, the fish began sizzling in the skillet and my mind soon fell away from unpleasant thoughts. The inviting aroma of freshly cooked trout began to fill the air of the cabin and before I knew it, Emery handed me a bowl of the delightful meat.

I quickly grabbed a whole fish with my hands and took an enormous bite. The old man watched as I chewed, slurped, and swallowed each mouthful of tender trout. Of all the food I had feasted upon in my lifetime, I reflected, this was by far the most savory. I quickly devoured the trout and was handed another.

When I had finished the second fish, Emery chuckled and handed me his bowl. "You need this more than I."

"Thank you," I said, and I took his bowl and proceeded to consume his meal too. When I was done I licked my fingers and wiped my face with my tunic. Emery handed me a horn of water and I gulped it down with haste. He filled it five more times and I sucked down every drop. Then he set the horn down upon the earthen floor and gazed directly into my eyes.

"Now tell me your story Winston Tabor, and I shall listen."

"How do you know my name?" I asked. "I don't remember giving it to you."

"Come now my lad, we both know who you are. There should be no beating around the bush. Tell me what happened—and tell me the truth."

I stared into the old man's shimmering blue eyes and I couldn't help but tell him everything I could recall about what took place on the day of my father's death. I explained to him how I met Shelby on my way home from the tavern and how he had informed me that my father was murdered. I told Emery how I ran into the forest to escape but somehow Cyrus had found me. I recounted how Cyrus had arrogantly admitted his guilt to me. Emery's eyes never left mine as I spoke and I knew they searched for truth. I could only hope he believed me. Then I went on further to describe how it was Cyrus who killed Hector and not I.

I continued talking even after telling the old man my story. I confessed to him how I drank too much and how I hadn't gotten along with my father even though he had been a kind and gentle lord. "My father loved me with all his heart and I disappointed him!" I cried. Tears rolled down my face and I felt my skin flushing from humiliation. I was ashamed for crying in front of Emery and I became uneasy. "Have you no wine? Have you no ale? How does a man live without such drink?" I clamored.

"Easier than a man who lives for it," Emery answered in a soft-spoken voice.

Wiping the tears from my face, I tried to comprehend what he had said, but my thoughts were cloudy and unclear.

"You'll feel better in a day or two. Your body's still not used to being without ale. You must rest now and we shall talk later."

After patting my head with his hand, Emery stood up and said, "I'll get more wood for the fire." Then he ambled to the door and opened it, but just before he stepped out he turned around. "If it helps you rest easier, I believe you," he said, and with a wink of his eye he stepped out and closed the door.

I laid back in bed and my mind became muddled. My skin felt sweaty and my nerves jumped with every pop and flash of the glowing fire. The talk of ale made me yearn for some and I wondered when the last time it was that I had gone a full day without drinking excessively before now—five, six years ago? I couldn't remember.

The door opened, startling me, and I quickly sat up in bed. Emery stepped in with a bundle of wood in his arms. "Didn't mean to frighten you, it's just me." He let the bundle go and it dropped to the floor with a thud.

When the old man's dog heard this, he raised his head, opened his eyes, and gave Emery an annoyed glance. Then he laid his head back down and closed his eyes again.

"Worthless mongrel! I don't know why I let him live here—he does no work! He can't hunt and he won't fetch. He doesn't even have a name. He just dragged his miserable self here one day begging for food and he's stayed ever since." Emery shrugged his shoulders. "Guess I'm just too nice. That's always been my problem though. I believe I was born in the wrong time—what with chivalry and knights and wars and such. A man's only respected if he's a knight who's good in battle or if he's a rich landowner. Ah, but here I am and here I stay."

Thinking of ale and not paying any attention to what the old man had said, I asked, "Emery, why do you have no ale? I know of no home, not even the poorest serf's that has no ale. It's not safe to drink fresh water. It needs to be mixed with oats and fermented to make it clean."

"Yes, in many towns and villages it's not safe, especially if it doesn't come from a deep well or a fresh stream, but out here in the forest it's pure. Anyway, even if I had wine or ale I wouldn't drink it."

"Why not?"

"Well, I'm what many fools call a drinkwater. They think of me as strange, but ale's no good for some men."

"What do you mean, no good?" I asked, genuinely curious of his reasoning.

"It brings out the devil in some men and takes their soul away," he answered staunchly. "I've seen many a good man ravaged by the drink. It sneaks up behind them and steals their minds. When all those around them can plainly see what's wrong, they themselves are blind to it. They never stop to think that it might be the ale causing most of their problems. Instead, they continue to pour it down their throats and blame their failures on their family and friends. A drunk's life is worse than death, for he's already dead and living in hell."

Emery's firm belief in what he was saying was obvious from the manner in which he spoke and I wanted to know why. "And you?" I questioned. "Why do you not drink? You seem like a rational man, you certainly have no more problems than the next."

"Ah yes, and that's why I don't touch the drink, so I can live a peaceful life." Emery's voice became soft and he spoke sincerely. "I'm one of those men—who if I should let it—would be overtaken by the drink and it would destroy me. I have no command over ale. The only way I can control my want for drink is to stay away from it. I can't even have one sip, for if I ever do, a moment later I'll be pouring it down my throat with no shame."

"But don't you ever long for ale or wine? How do you celebrate during holidays or feasts?"

"Those are some of the hardest times for me, though I've not celebrated or feasted with anyone in years. During those celebrations that I have attended, I constantly reminded myself of how much happier I was without drink than I was with it. Also, I am always aware that if I have but one taste of the vile liquid, all I have gained will be lost."

"You make it sound so easy."

"But it is not. A man who vows to never drink again must reach deep within himself, for if he doesn't put all his heart and spirit into his vow, he will fail. But if he does fail, he must try again and again. Once he does finally free himself from the shackles of drink, he must never let down his guard. For the rest of his life he must keep a constant vigil on his want for ale. Especially during the most trying times of his life, when it's easier to reach for a tankard of wine than to face the truth."

Emery turned away and began to stoke the dying fire. The light flickered upon the side of his face distorting his image and complexion. Smoke twirled around him and he appeared as if in a dream. As I watched him, his words echoed in my ears and a hundred thoughts began whirling around in my head. Maybe I was one of those men that Emery spoke of? Maybe I was like the old man himself? Maybe I was destined to be a drinkwater?

*   *   *

For the next day and a half I went in and out of sleep. My body trembled and sweat poured from my skin as I became accustomed to not having any ale to drink. Every now and then the old man served me soup or gave me water. He made me take his medicine and if I vomited it up, he'd mix up another batch and force me to drink it.

A few days later, in the afternoon, Emery and I had supper together. We ate salted pork and shared a meager loaf of bread that he had procured in my village of Dereham a day earlier. It was raining outside and I heard it pattering upon the thatched roof. The only light was that provided by the glowing fire that drew strange shadows upon the walls of the cabin.

By now I was gaining my strength back and though my wounds still hurt, especially upon movement, they no longer wept. I had no idea if the old man's medicine had actually worked or if it was an act of God that had let me live. No matter what the reason was, I was grateful to both of them. Still, I was weak and needed more rest, but I felt my full recovery was inevitable.

After our meal, we drank tea sweetened with honey. Emery told me that he was a beekeeper and maintained a number of hives within the forest. His honey was his livelihood and he traded it for other provisions at the markets in the nearby towns and villages. He kept his jugs of honey in a tiny storage shed outside.

As we chatted and sipped the warm sweet tea, I rested on the old man's straw bed. Emery placed himself next to me on a stool and then reached beneath his bed and tossed something onto my lap. It was my wallet.

"Here," he said, "this was in your possession when I found you in the grove of trees. You carry half a year's wages in your handbag for a man like me. Ah, what I would give to be young and foolish again!"

"Ah," I said, mimicking Emery, "what I would give to be old and wise like you!"

We both began to chuckle. A twinkle shone from Emery's eyes and he appeared twenty years younger. At that moment I felt very close to the old man and I had a sudden urge to know why he believed the story I had told him.

"Emery, why do you trust so freely the words I have told you about what happened to my father in Dereham? How do you know I'm not lying and that in the middle of the night I might kill you and rob your home?"

A great thunderous roar of laughter poured out from Emery's throat. "Ha ha ha ha ha! Steal? Rob? Ha ha ha ha ha! And what would I have that you might steal? An old stool? My bed? My old dog? Ha ha ha ha ha!"

As he cackled, I began to laugh too. The old man smacked his right hand upon his thigh and tears welled up in both our eyes. It wasn't anything that funny, it was just that we were both in high spirits; me for knowing I would fully recover and he for having company about him. Finally our laughter died down and I asked him again why he believed my story.

This time he answered in utter seriousness. "I believe you because I too have been dealt a bad hand by this Cyrus Everett of whom you speak."

"How do you know him? What did he do to you?" I questioned.

"What I say now must never leave this room," he replied.

"I promise," I vowed, placing my hand upon my chest.

"As a younger man, I used to live in Dereham. Your father was very young then and his father was lord of the village. Cyrus Everett was the son of a wealthy merchant who lived in London and he was sent to your grandfather's castle as a small boy. He became your father's companion and eventually his squire once your father was knighted. Cyrus soon learned that he could use his relationship with your father for personal gain. When your grandfather died, your father appointed Cyrus bailiff. That position he abused profusely and always did."

"Yes," I nodded in agreement, "I've heard the stories, but I never thought they were true. Now I believe them."

"Besides taxing the citizens illegally," continued Emery, "Cyrus also loans money. That's not wrong in its self, for we both know many a friend who has lent another money. But Cyrus charges a fee—what he calls interest—besides the amount he lends. We both know that's illegal and the church would excommunicate him if they knew about it."

"The devil!" I exclaimed.

"There is still worse to be heard," said Emery in a now somber voice and far away look in his eyes. "Once, a young serf named Jared Quincy owed Cyrus money. I was there at Jared's shanty when Cyrus came to collect. Cyrus was in a foul mood and he'd had a bit too much to drink. Jared had no money to pay him, so in a wrath of fury Cyrus cut him down right then and there in front of me. Just minutes after, Cyrus realized he'd made a mistake. Even he knew that any man, be he serf or gentry, was part of God's domain and that he had no right to take Jared's life. Cyrus also knew that the county steward would be sent to investigate the murder and if the story was told as it truly had happened, Cyrus would have lost his head."

As I watched Emery tell his tale, I noticed he was beginning to tremble. In his clear blue eyes I thought I saw a tear. He stood up and turned away from me and wiped his eyes.

"My throat's too dry," he said as he stood. "I need some water. Would you like some too?"

I shook my head and watched the old man pick a clean horn off of the wall and dip it in a pail of water.

"Well, what happened? Why didn't the county steward have him arrested? Why wasn't he beheaded long ago so he would never have had the chance to kill my father?"

Emery turned and gazed at me. He appeared distraught. He lifted the horn of water to his lips and took a gulp. Then he poured some of the water into his hands and splashed it onto his face.

"I'm the reason he was never arrested," Emery said softly. "Cyrus paid me off. I was a drunkard and I needed money. My mind was controlled by the ale, though I know that's no excuse." Emery cleared his throat and took another sip of water. "The county steward investigated and Cyrus and I told him that Jared had attacked Cyrus first. We said that Jared had swung an axe at Cyrus when he was asked about the money he owed."

Appearing pale, Emery knelt down and faced one of the walls of the cabin where a miniature iron cross was hung. "Father, please forgive me," he whispered as he folded his hands together and a tear rolled down his cheek.

I gazed at the old man kneeling in front of the crucifix and I understood how he felt. I too had done things with ale on my breath that I had regretted later, though none had been as terrible as this. I reached my left hand out and placed it on his shoulder. He took my hand in his and squeezed it tight.

Then Emery turned his face toward me and his eyes met mine. I could see the reflection of the fire dancing within his pupils. "You must stay off of the drink and grow strong," he said. "You shall act and dress like a peasant. If anyone asks, you are my nephew and your name is Jacob Fulton. You've come from London because your parents have passed away. And you shall stay here with me until you are fully recovered."

"And what of Cyrus Everett?" I asked. "When shall I extract my revenge? When shall I kill the pig?"

With a strange distant look in his eyes, the hermit quietly replied. "We shall see, we shall see."

CHAPTER THREE

Nearly three months had passed since my father's murder and my near fatal encounter with Cyrus Everett. During that time I'd gone into the small town of Cawston twice for supplies that the old man and I had needed.

Cawston was a village about the same size as Dereham and it was located nearly six miles to the east, across the stream from the old man's cottage. Dereham laid to the west.

There was a modest tavern in Cawston that I had to pass on my way to the market place. Unfortunately, on both occasions, the temptation had been too great and on my way back from trading I had stopped in front of the alehouse.

Maybe I'll have just one mug of ale, I had thought. The next minute I'd found myself gulping down mug after mug of the frothy brew until late into the evening. Eventually, I had stumbled back to Emery's cabin drunk and disappointed with myself.

When I awoke feeling rotten on the following mornings, I was surprised that the old man never uttered a bad word to me. He would say only one thing, "When you fall off of your horse, you should get back on it." And both times I had, though I began to wonder if I would ever keep myself away from ale and the like. I knew I felt much better being sober than I did when I was drunk, yet both times when I had had the opportunity to drink, I couldn't resist it.

My will was weak, but still an urge within my heart continued to grow with each new day. That desire told me I had to keep away from the drink, for if I didn't, it would be the death of me. I had to keep trying.

*   *   *

It was a pleasant day for late winter and the sun was shinning brightly as I stepped out of the old man's shanty. A light breeze blew from the south and whisked my hair around my face. I felt good for the first time in a long while. My wounds were healed completely and my body was growing strong.

I began hiking up along the stream that flowed beside Emery's cabin. According to the old man, the stream eventually emptied into the Wensum River and then continued on to the sea. I had followed this trail several times in the past month. In my hands I carried a fishing rod made from a fresh alder branch and at the end of the rod was some thin but strong thread to act as line. A bent iron nail was all Emery had for a fishhook. Simple, but it worked.

Rambling along the path, I enjoyed listening to the sound of the water as it twirled and bubbled past me. I inhaled deeply and smelled the fresh earthly odor of the forest. It had been an unusually warm winter and the undergrowth was coming back to life again as if it were already spring. I had never noticed before, but the forest was a magnificent sight to behold. Above me I heard the pounding of a woodpecker on the trunk of an old elm tree. Then suddenly, a heron flew before me and dipped its protracted beak down into the swift waters of the stream and snatched up a stout fish. How wonderful, I marveled, even with all its hardship and cruelty, the world still had its bright and beautiful times.

As I enjoyed my stroll through the woodland, my mind unhappily wandered onto a trail of less pleasant thoughts. One of those thoughts was the dark image of what I had overheard the last time I had been in Cawston. It was only a rumor spoken by peasants at the market, but I knew that rumors were often based on fact. The idle talk was that the widowed Lady Acacia Tabor, my mother, would soon be wedded and that her new lord would be Cyrus Everett. How could this be? I had wondered over and over again in the last few days. Why would my mother marry the man who killed her husband? Does she still not know the truth? "What a conniving serpent—that blackguard Cyrus!" I muttered to myself as I passed the brambles and bracken that grew along the water's edge.

Nearing the fishing hole, my thoughts fell away from Cyrus. Though the destruction of him was always in the back of my mind, I knew I was not prepared to extract my revenge from him yet. I had to wait until the right moment, after months of preparation and planning, but first I had to deal with the present. And the present was quite confusing.

There I was wearing a peasant's tunic when I was actually the son of a Lord. My real name was Winston Tabor and yet I called myself Jacob Fulton. And the old man—who was he really? He was too bright to be just a simple peasant. He was also the kindest stranger I had ever met, and yet I felt that he was hiding something from me. I had no inkling of what it was, but I knew it was something.

Soon I arrived at Emery's favorite fishing hole, which he had shown me four weeks before. The stream ran fairly straight in this stretch of the forest, except for one area where an immense boulder blocked its path. The natural flow of the water was obstructed and it swirled around the rock creating a deep calm pool. It was a good place for the fish to stop and rest before continuing on their way upstream.

Gazing into the clear water, I saw a number of fat trout swimming beneath the smooth surface. I sat down on a mossy rock and stretched my legs out. Grabbing the hilt of the humble sword, which Emery had given to me to use, I pulled it from its sheath. It was old and worn, but it was better than no weapon at all. I couldn't carry my own sword, for it would have appeared suspicious for a peasant, such as I was pretending to be, to be carrying as valuable a weapon as the one my father had given me. I jabbed the tip into the moist earth and pulled back a clod of dirt. Three worms immediately tried to squirm back into the ground and I picked up the fattest one and stuck it on the bent nail. I tossed the line into the water and waited.

Though I could have been arrested for poaching, as it was illegal to use the forest for hunting and fishing, the old man had assured me that the king's foresters rarely ventured into this area of the woods. If they did, it was quiet enough that I'd likely be able to hear them coming in time for me to hide. If by chance I was caught, the king's courts could be harsh and I'd likely lose an ear or a finger for my first offense. For larger animals such as a deer or fox, a man could lose his hand. If it were a second offense, he may well lose his head. Luckily, I'd never seen anyone near this area in the last few weeks, except that is, for her. And she was there again today.

She was young about my age with long blond hair, and from what I could see, quite a pleasing figure. I had never observed her up close, for she always appeared downstream and across the water from me. She always carried a full basket of clothes and linens that she daintily washed in the stream.

I had hoped to meet her sometime as I hiked to or from Emery's fishing hole, but she had never appeared at the stream till I had already arrived and was fishing. I found myself too shy to actually go down and say hello to her. Instead I could only watch with great wonder as her body moved, as only a woman's does, to her duties of the wash.

I don't believe she had ever noticed me fishing; though she easily could have had she set her eyes in the right direction. I knew it was improper to watch her without her knowledge, but I couldn't keep my eyes off of her. She was a ray of sunlight in the dark forest of my strange life.

Suddenly and unexpectedly, a shower of water splashed upon my face and I quickly turned my head away from the girl and toward the small pool. My eyes caught the tail of what appeared to be a huge trout diving back down into the water. The fish jumped again and went straight up into the air. I watched it and, though it hung in the air for but an instant, it seemed like minutes went by. Its great body twisted back and forth and its scaly skin glistened in the sunlight. Beads of water sparkled as they sprayed from the silvery speckled mass. It was the largest trout I had ever seen.

As it turned and fell back toward the water, I saw my line dangling from its mouth. Realizing I had the fish hooked, a rush of excitement rippled through my body and I grabbed my pole and stood up quickly. Just as I began to pull the fish in, I slipped on some moss and nearly fell into the water. While steadying myself, the great fish shot out of the stream like an arrow. It pulled on my rod and sent me toppling over. Turning this way and that, I tried to regain my balance, but I was too far out of control.

I fell backward and head down into the pool. With my eyes wide open, I saw only bubbles in a clear world of liquid. After realizing what had happened, my instincts had me vertical within seconds and I popped my head up above the surface. An instant later the shock of the cold water hit me, allowing me to take only short quick gulps of air.

I began swimming toward the bank that was only a few feet away, but the current in the pool was much stronger than I could have imagined. I wasn't making any headway. All of a sudden, I was swept past the huge stone that blocked much of the course of the stream. My body was tossed back and forth and then I was sucked beneath the water.

Spinning around and around, I felt helpless. There was nothing I could do but let my body go with the current. My arms, legs, and head smashed and bumped mercilessly into the rocks strewn upon the floor of the stream.

Luckily, the rough part of the current quickly ended and I was left treading water while drifting downstream. I saw no sign of my pole or the wonderful fish that was nearly mine.

What I did see was the face of a beautiful girl, more brilliant than I could have ever imagined. But what was that I heard? Was it laughter? Yes it was, and it was coming from the lovely girl who stood before me on the bank of the stream.

I peered at her with a contemptuous gaze and she must have felt pity for me. "I'm sorry," she said. "I didn't mean to laugh, but I saw the whole display."

"A man almost drowns and you think it's funny?" I asked as I waded into shore.

"I'm sorry," she repeated. "I didn't mean to hurt your feelings."

"That's okay," I replied as my displeasure was quickly replaced with shyness and I stepped out of the cold water. The girl stood before me wearing a wool kirtle that flowed down to her feet. On her center was tied a belt of rope that fit snugly around her petite waist. She wore her shimmering blond hair in plaits, keeping it up and out of her lovely blue eyes—eyes that sang as I gazed into them.

"My name is Meranda, Meranda Cayton."

"I'm Win—Jacob Fulton."

"Do you prefer to be called Win or Jacob?"

"Call me Jacob," I said with a sigh of relief. She was so beautiful that I had nearly forgotten to use my assumed name.

"Do you live around here?" she asked. "I haven't seen you before, except for the few times you've been fishing up there." She pointed upstream toward the pool where I'd just been.

"You've seen me up there before? Why didn't you say hello?"

"I don't know, why didn't you?" she asked with her eyes gazing toward the ground. "I know you were watching me."

"I was not," I quickly denied, suddenly feeling ashamed as I stood there dripping wet.

"Well, if you were, it's okay. I watched you when you weren't looking too." She giggled.

I laughed nervously and said, "Meranda is a pretty name."

"Thank you, Jacob is a nice name too."

I felt the skin on my face and neck flush and then a silence filled the air. I wasn't sure of what to say to her. I couldn't recall a time when I had been alone with a girl without having first warmed my belly with drink. Finally I asked, "Do you know the old man who lives down stream about a mile or so? He has a cabin and tends bees."

"Yes, I've seen him and spoke with him before, but I don't know his name."

"He's my uncle and his name is Emery Fulton. I live with him in the forest."

"That's strange," she said, "you would have thought we'd have met before now."

"I've only lived with him for a few months. You see, my parents were both stricken with a sudden illness and passed on. I had to move here from London to stay with my uncle. He's the only family I know."

"I'm so sorry," she said.

"It's okay," I replied, and then I asked, "where do you live Meranda?"

"Up this trail here, about a quarter of a mile." She gestured toward a path that led perpendicular to the stream opposite the side from where I had come. "My father has a few strips of land which he rents from Baron Wellington."

"So your father is a farmer?"

"Yes, he grows wheat and peas mostly. His name is Roger Cayton, perhaps you've heard of him?"

"No, I haven't, but as you know I haven't been around here long."

"I hope you don't mind me asking," Meranda spoke, "but how come your uncle doesn't live in any of the villages nearby? I've always thought that only outlaws or hermits live back in the forest."

I pondered her question for a moment. "I don't know, to tell you the truth. I guess in a way he is a hermit. He goes to town for the things he needs but otherwise he keeps to himself here in the woodland. I guess he likes being alone." As I uttered those words to Meranda I thought again about Emery and how little I really knew about him.

A hush settled in on our conversation again and I gazed at her with searching eyes. I wanted to say something more; something to impress her, but no words would come to my lips.

"I must be going," she said, "and you should get back to your uncle's. Look, you're shivering."

I glanced down at myself and realized she was right. I was shivering. Then Meranda began to gather the clothes she had washed and I asked, "will I see you again?"

"Yes, if you'd like. Maybe you can come and meet my parents. They love to have visitors, especially people who have come from such a far away place as London. I've never been to London, but maybe you can tell me all about it sometime."

"Yes, I'd like too," I said. "Will you be here tomorrow?"

"I'm not sure, I've done most of the wash today. I'll have to see."

"I'll be here." I blurted out.

She smiled. "Good-bye. Maybe I'll see you tomorrow."

"I hope so," I replied as she scampered away.

She was so beautiful, I marveled. I'd seen her only a few times and I'd spoken to her only once, but I felt as though I had known her for a lifetime. How could my feelings be so strong? She was but a peasant girl and I was the son of a Lord.

I stepped back into the shallow part of the stream and crossed over. Peering back at the path that led to her home, I could only hope that she felt just a little for me of what I felt for her.

The walk home was not as tedious and cold as it could have been and when I reached the old man's cabin, he was outside spading his small garden. It needed to be ready for spring to sow the few things that he grew himself. I caught his eyes and he turned to me.

"Ah my lad, you've returned, but I see no fish in hand, nor pole or line either. You're soaking from head to toe. Decided to go swimming huh?" He laughed thoroughly.

"I'm cold and I'm going inside to start a fire! I'll tell you about it later!"

"Alright," he said, shaking his head and laughing.

As I entered the cabin I stepped over the old dog that lay in the doorway. I reached down and patted his head and he immediately rolled over on his back to have his tummy stroked. Since the old man had no name for the hound I called him Jiggers. I'd even taught him two commands, to come when called and to sit. I knew little about the beasts in general, for I'd never taken much interest in the dogs my father had owned, but the hound was friendly and I enjoyed his company. Emery liked him too, despite his complaints about the dog's laziness.

I strode over to the hearth and blew on the coals left over from the morning's fire. Grabbing a piece of dry oak from the woodpile, I set it upon the glowing embers and began to undress. Within minutes the fire was blazing and I was dressed in some old clothes of Emery's. Warm and dry, I perched myself on a stool near the crackling flames and my thoughts focused on Meranda.

The door opened and Emery stepped into the dimly lit room. "Get us some bread my lad, and a bit of bacon. I'll make some tea and we'll have a bite to eat."

I retrieved some bacon from the food locker. The locker was basically a chest buried in the earth in a corner of the cabin and it was intended to keep food cool. I opened the top of it and pulled out the meat.

Though the bacon was heavily salted to preserve it, it had been stored all winter and it was beginning to take on a rancid odor. We cooked it thoroughly in a skillet over the fire, yet it was still a good thing that Emery had plenty of onion and garlic sauces to disguise the flavor.

As Emery and I ate and sipped tea, I told him of the events that had occurred earlier in the morning. The old man laughed when I described my accidental plunge into the stream and how I lost my pole. I told him about the girl named Meranda and I asked him if he knew of her.

"Ah, the one with the long blond hair?"

I nodded.

"Yes, I've spoken to her. She's a peasant girl and her father's a farmer, but that's all I know."

"She's beautiful." I said.

"Ah, so your heart is beating like a bird. Faster and faster till it skips a beat," said Emery chuckling.

I smiled, "I'm going to see her again tomorrow."

"Fine my boy, just bring home some fish this time and be wary. Love can put you off guard and if the king's foresters get a hold of you, no telling what will happen."

"Don't worry," I replied, "I'll watch out." Then I directed the subject back to Meranda. "Emery? You know I'm a nobleman's son. Is it wrong for me to befriend a peasant girl? Isn't my blood different than hers?"

"Listen," the old man said, "you may take me for a fool, but I believe the gentry, the peasants, and the serfs are all the same in flesh and blood. The only difference is wealth and knowledge. Perhaps someday everyone will be considered equals. Probably not in my lifetime nor in yours, but hopefully someday."

"That's a good thought," I replied as I sipped my tea and pictured Meranda standing by the stream as she had earlier that day. I couldn't wait to see her the next day if she could make it. I hoped she could.

As if reading my mind, Emery spoke. "Just remember Winston, or have you forgotten? As a peasant, she's not looking for a husband. The man she'll marry will be chosen by her father."

With those words my heart sunk in my chest. I'd forgotten that peasant women don't choose their own husbands, or most noblewomen for that matter. The only way I could ever hope to marry her would be to regain my position as a nobleman and ask her father for her hand in marriage. But there was one obstacle, the fat pig of a man named Cyrus Everett.

My face turned red and my blood ran hot as I pictured Cyrus. While I lived the life of a peasant, he sat and got fatter off of the wealth of my mother. What an evil and vile man he is!

"Don't look so distressed," said Emery. "You've met her but once. Why do young men fall in love so fast?"

"You're right, I shall try not to think about her so much. What happens shall happen. She's but a girl anyway."

Emery stood up and slapped his hand on my leg. "Good my lad, now let's go. We've got work to do."

We went outside and for the rest of the day we weeded and spaded the old man's garden. As the sun went down and the forest's trees drew extended shadows, we trudged inside to the comfort of the cottage. Both of us were tired from the long day, so we broke bread, gave thanks for our blessings, and retired for the evening. Emery slept on his own bed while I laid myself down in a soft pile of straw in a corner of the cabin.

The next morning I awoke before daylight. Having slept in my clothes, as all but the gentry do, I went directly outside and down to the stream. I washed my face and hands, shaved, and filled a pail of water to bring up to the cabin. When I returned, Emery was up and he had restarted the fire. He also had a tiny loaf of bread on the table for us. We made three signs of the cross in honor of the trinity and said a prayer. Then we ate our bread and drank some tea.

After breakfast, I stepped outside and the morning sun was just breaking out between a handful of clouds and illuminated the forest. Being glad to leave the smoky confines of the cabin, I inhaled a deep breath of fresh air. The birds chirped and whistled which accompanied the babbling stream to create a wonderful melody. I stood there for a moment listening and then I ambled over to a nearby alder tree and cut off a long thin shoot. This was to be my new fishing rod and it was perfect. It was straight, strong, and flexible. Emery had given me some more strong thread and another bent nail so I was ready to be on my way.

Lightly and happily I strolled along the footpath leading to the fishing hole. Not very excited about catching fish, I was really looking forward to seeing Meranda. A good night's sleep had returned me to my senses and in the back of my mind I knew nothing lasting would likely come of our meeting each other, but she was a pretty girl and I was a young man. It was nice just to be with a girl of my age, even if she was only a peasant.

In fact, I reasoned, it might even be better that she is a peasant. Maybe her interests won't be of meaningless drivel like so many of the noble women. Too often the gentry are caught up in worthless impressions and wasteful actions just to prove how noble they are.

The weather didn't appear as nice as the day before and a smattering of dark clouds hovered over the treetops. The wind was beginning to pick up and I suspected a storm was brewing, but it didn't dampen my spirit at all.

As I approached the site where Meranda had been the day before, my feet stepped faster. I rounded a bend in the path and there she was, washing clothes as before, but this time something was different. She appeared more fair and lovely than ever. Her kirtle was made of a finer material than the one she'd worn the previous day and her lengthy blond hair was curled with a bright yellow bow tied into it. Had she done this for me?

"Hello Meranda!" I called across the stream.

"Hello Jacob!" She smiled at me brightly.

I scurried up to the bank and realized I couldn't get across unless I waded through the water.

Meranda laughed. "Aren't you going to swim across like yesterday?"

I grinned and began taking off my leather shoes and stockings. I pulled up my breeches and stepped into the water. It was frigid and I was glad that only my feet and calves had to be immersed. The rocks were sharp on my tender feet and the going was slow, but soon I found myself on the other side.

"You look quite a bit different when you're not drenched—better I should think."

"Why thank you," I replied, catching a glimpse of her rich blue eyes. Then, although feeling a bit bashful, I forced myself to return a compliment. "You look very pretty today."

Blushing, Meranda twisted her hands together, placed one foot in front of the other, and peered down at the ground. "Thank you Jacob."

I felt a wave of joy rush through me.

"I've more wash to do today, would you like to help?" she asked.

"Yes, just let me set up my pole and toss the line in the water. Maybe I can catch my supper at the same time."

"You best keep an eye out for the king's men! They'll have one of your fingers or worse yet, if you're caught!"

"Don't worry, I've never seen them around here. Have you?"

"Once that I can remember."

"When was that?" I asked.

"A couple of years ago, about a mile east of here, they caught a serf who had poached a wild pig."

"Really? What happened?"

"Well, the whole county had had a bad harvest that year and everyone was having a hard time finding enough to eat through the following winter. Many of the sick and old died."

"Yes, I remember that year," I replied.

"How do you remember? You're from London aren't you?"

"I mean I heard about it from my uncle. Please go on. What happened to the poor man?"

"The man lived in the village of Dereham, so I'm not too sure of the details. Everyone presumed the poacher would lose his head. But what I heard was that Lord Tabor, the master of the town, took matters into his own hands and let the man go free. I guess he felt sorry for the poor soul and his family. He must've been a good lord to serve." She paused for a moment and then spoke again. "Terrible what his wicked son did to him."

"Yes, terrible." I agreed, wanting to say more.

Meranda did have a reason to be worried about my poaching fish, but it wasn't an infrequent occurrence for peasants to steal small game or fish from the forest. Her own father probably hunted squirrels and rabbits to help supplement their need for meat. It was the larger animals one must be most worried about stealing. I reassured her that it was only a few scant fish I wanted and that I wasn't going to stalk a deer.

For the rest of the morning I helped her with the wash. We talked about the weather and how it appeared as though it might storm. She asked me about the city of London and what it was like. I told her as much as I knew, from what I'd heard from travelers and from what my tutors had taught me. However, it did make me feel quite uneasy lying to Meranda.

The wash seemed scarcely like actually doing work. We laughed and joked with each other and the morning went by swiftly. It was like a wonderful dream hearing her voice and gazing into her eyes as we talked. Her body moved with such grace, as if she were an angel dancing on a breeze. Her blonde hair fluttered in the wind and whipped about her vibrant face. She was so beautiful, I thought over and over again. I wished I could have touched her or held her in my arms for but an instant.

"Jacob! Jacob! You have a fish on your line!"

I glanced up from my daydreaming and found she was right. There was a hefty trout on my line and it had almost pulled my pole into the stream. Grabbing the rod, I tugged up on it fast and the fish came flying out of the water, slapping me across my face.

Meranda started laughing and I began to chuckle too. I wiped the fish slime off of my cheek and nodded my head back and forth with a comical expression on my face. Meranda laughed even harder.

By noon, rain started pouring from the thick clouds that had gathered overhead. Meranda had to get back to her father's cottage. She thanked me for helping her with the wash and we agreed to see each other again in two days. I strolled back to Emery's cabin with a light heart and three fish.

When I got back to the shanty, Emery wasn't around. I figured he was off tending his beehives or foraging for mushrooms or anything else for that matter. I set the trout upon the bare table and went down to the river to get some water. When I returned, I cleaned the fish and fed the entrails to Jiggers who licked his jowls in delight. Then I placed the trout in a pail of water to keep them cool until the old man returned for supper.

Outside, the garden was nearly ready for sowing, but Emery didn't want to plant anything until he was sure there wouldn't be another frost. Since there was nothing for me to do, I laid down on the old man's bed to rest for a bit.

While lying on the bed, I pulled the old sword that Emery had given me out of its scabbard and turned it around in my hands. It was worn and discolored with a few rust spots scattered upon its surface. The double-edged blade was pitted and not very sharp. I remembered that the sword my father had given me was somewhere in the cabin. I hadn't felt it in my hands since that dreadful day over three months earlier. Where would the old man have hidden it? I pondered.

I let my eyes wander around the one room shack. Like most peasants' homes there was scant furniture in the dwelling and certainly none adequate enough to hide a sword. A small table, a chair, two stools and a chest were the only large possessions Emery owned besides his bed, and his bed was but a few boards and a mattress of straw.

Underneath the mattress I quickly thought—that could be the only place to hide a sword. I jumped off of the bed and turned over the cushion. There it was, clean and shiny, sitting next to the clothes I'd been wearing when Emery had found me. The old man must have polished it and tried to clean the blood from my garments, though my clothes were still badly stained. Then I noticed another blade halfway sticking out from under the turned up fold of the mattress. I reached down and picked it up.

It was an impressive piece of weaponry, the likes of which I'd never seen before. It shimmered brightly in the dull glow of the cabin. Its hilt was elaborately decorated with delicate impressions of symbols unknown to me. It was obviously not from this region and likely not even from Christendom.

"Fine piece of steel she is!"

I turned around and there stood Emery in the doorway. I was surprised and I felt like a child caught with his hand in the honey pot. "I'm sorry Emery. I didn't mean to trespass upon your private possessions."

Like always, the old man assured me that I'd done no wrong and said, "Don't worry my boy. You've caused no harm. She's a beauty though, eh?"

"Sure is. I've never seen another one like it. Where did you get it?"

"It's from a part of my life I cherish most. It was given to me by a courtly prince while traveling in China."

Amazed and unbelieving, I placed myself down on a stool. "Why haven't you mentioned this before?"

"You may not understand," he replied, settling himself on a chair and ignoring my question. "It was the pinnacle of my existence. Traveling to China and learning their customs, especially their mode of combat, was more than a knight could have dreamt."

The old man, a knight? Could it really be? That would explain a lot, I reasoned. "Why did you not tell me you're a knight?"

"You never asked," he chuckled, "but I've been meaning to tell you, and I guess it's time I did. It's a long story, so I'll try to make it short, but let me make some tea first."

After a few minutes, the two of us were nestled by the flickering fire holding steaming horns of tea in our hands.

"Okay Emery," I said, "now tell me your story."

"Well," he replied, "I don't really know where to begin. I used to believe that battle was the most glorious expression of chivalry there was. After returning from my second journey to China, I dreamed of using my skills in combat for admirable causes, like King Arthur and his famous knights."

"Your second journey to China? How many times did you go there? What did you do there?"

"No my lad," replied the old man, "I will tell you about China later. First, I must tell you this. As I had said, I returned home to England and dreamt of using my skills for an admirable cause. Instead, I found myself fighting the Welsh for King Edward the First. We conquered and won and when we came home, we were treated like royalty. Feasts were given in our honor and minstrels sang of our victories. But I felt none of the glory I'd so duly wanted. I felt only grief and remorse for massacring the peasants and burning their villages in the name of England. They were people like you and I. They meant us no harm and caused us no trouble. It was only greed and ignorance which led us to conquer Wales, not a Godly command."

I gaped at Emery in astonishment, but I knew he told the truth. What I had been taught about the Welsh as a child had been lies.

Beads of sweat dripped from the old man's forehead and he looked pale and tired, but he also appeared relieved, as though a heavy weight had been lifted from his chest.

Emery spoke again. "I became disillusioned with chivalry and all it stood for. I began seeking life's answers at the bottom of an ale horn and I vowed to never fight again. I saw chivalry and knighthood as an occupation of death and greed. I thought nothing good could ever come from it, only grief and sorrow. So I gave it all up—chivalry, knighthood, and even people. Eventually, after nearly dying from the overindulgence of drink, I thankfully gave that up too. Then I moved out here to the woodland where I thought I could find peace from humanity. But because of you and your situation, lately I've had to rethink many things. I have found that I was wrong about fighting and chivalry, for like most things you can find both good and evil in them.

Sometimes you must fight for what is right. I can no longer live in naivety, as I believed I could. Out here in the forest it is peaceful, but no matter how peaceful it is where one lives, one must be prepared and ready to fight against what is evil."

As the old man spoke, I listened intently and for the rest of that afternoon and well into the night he talked about the strange and wonderful life he had lived. He told me about his travels to the Far East with a man named Marco Polo and how he had been taught many unique fighting skills while he was there. He recounted all of the vicissitudes he had experienced, but not once did he boast. His modesty and truthfulness brought him closer to my heart than ever before. I had always known there was something special about him and that night I found out what it was. Also, I came to realize that I loved the old man like a father.

When it was late and Emery had finished speaking, I asked, "Would it be possible to teach me your skills with the sword?"

There was a long drawn-out pause. The crackling of the fire grew louder and louder until it seemed, to me, to be the intensity of a forest fire. I nearly thought the cabin would burst into flames at any moment. Then, after an arduous muffled sigh, the old man spoke. "I shall teach you."

CHAPTER FOUR

It was the middle of June. Over four months had come and gone since Emery began showing me his skills with the sword.

My thoughts were growing clear without ale to cloud them and I was gaining confidence in myself. In the last month, I'd gone to Cawston once alone and once with the old man. Neither time had I let the temptation for drink entice me into the tavern. No longer would ale possess the reins of my spirit. I was becoming a man in control of my actions and my destiny.

But while I was becoming physically and spiritually better, a disgraceful episode had taken place in my village. The news of this sorrowful event had been brought to me by Emery and had been foretold by the previous rumor I had heard. The old man had learned from a few townsfolk in Cawston that my mother, Lady Acacia, had wedded Cyrus Everett—only seven months after my father's murder.

How dishonorable and ignoble could my mother be? I had wondered. I knew in my heart that what she had done was wrong and there was no excuse for it. Still, my mother had always been a good and caring woman, so I was convinced that Cyrus had been the main instigator. He must have played upon all of her emotions, which undoubtedly had been left tattered after the death of my father. Cyrus wanted only one thing, and now he had it, to be Lord of Dereham. I felt shame and pity for my mother, but because of my love for her I did find forgiveness.

During this same period, Meranda and I were becoming close friends. I had even enjoyed supper with her parents, telling them all I knew of London, as though I had really lived there. They received me fairly well, albeit I believed Meranda's father was not too pleased with our friendship. Rationally, he surmised that nothing good could come of it. Her beauty would be wasted if he were to choose me, a landless peasant, as her future husband. It was almost certainly obvious to everyone in her family that our companionship could only lead to trouble.

The weather had been generally wet during the past four months and the stream near the old man's cabin had twice nearly flooded his modest garden. In the garden we had sown peas, beans, cabbage, turnips, and onions. The plants had sprouted a few weeks earlier and were now growing heartily especially since the sun had recently decided to visit us more frequently in the past week and a half.

The sun was now blazing brilliantly in the eastern morning sky as Emery and I stood on the grassy bank of the stream near his cottage. The wind was warm and blew lightly across my face as the old man, with his sword in hand, came at me with a jab to my abdomen. Facing him, I put my left foot back and turned my body toward the point of attack. At the same time I forced his sword away from me with the blade in my right hand. I stepped back and Emery held up his sword and brought it down upon me. As he had taught me, I stepped into the oncoming blow while raising my sword up to block it. My right leg was planted straight back to anchor my body and my left leg was bent and ready to pivot. I prevented the strike with the sword in my right hand and I punched his chest with my left hand.

"Good show Winston! You've got a great stance and the makings of a fine swordsman! Remember though, the heat of battle is quite different from practice. Rage and fear determine a large part of who wins or loses."

"I'm aware of that," I replied, "and the one who controls his emotions has the upper hand."

"You learn fast my lad, but there is much more for you to master before you set out on your own."

I nodded in agreement. "Emery? Why don't you use a shield? Wouldn't it be safer to have some sort of cover to deflect oncoming strikes?"

"Shields are awkward and heavy, putting a man off balance. Using your blade as a shield works better, as you have just done. It requires less strength and it is easier to move about."

"You're right. It does seem simpler than when I practiced using a shield as a squire. Of course I never learned any moves except for jabbing and hacking."

"Precisely. That's sword fighting in Christendom. There's no flow or variance. It's only hacking and thrusting. Once you know that, you need only to figure out ways to prevent those attacks. Then you can use the force of your opponent against him. Usually, after he's attacked and you've deflected, he's in a vulnerable position. That's when you strike."

What Emery said made sense. "What about armor and chain mail? Do they use that in China?"

"Yes, they use a few plates of armor and chain mail to cover the most vital parts of the body, but they don't weigh themselves down with whole suits. When fighting the Welsh I saw many a man in full suits of armor knocked from their mounts in the thick of battle. Many were so tired they couldn't stand and some even suffocated."

"Truthfully?" I questioned.

"Yes, truly, but don't misunderstand me. In a tournament, using a lance, you need at least a shield if not armor too. Or if you're assaulting a castle you'll need a mantelet to protect you from whatever they hurl upon you. What I teach you is mainly for combat on foot."

"I understand," I replied.

We practiced awhile longer until the morning was gone. Then we went inside, prayed, broke bread with honey, and washed it all down with horns of water. Jiggers, who was hungry also, enjoyed a mixture of stale bread and bacon that had gone bad. He wagged his tail in elation and licked his jowls when he was done.

"Worthless mutt." Emery groaned, though a twinkle of delight shone in his eyes contradicting the words he spoke. He reached down and patted the dog's head and Jiggers licked his hand with gratefulness.

After eating, the old man went outside to spend the afternoon tending his bees and weeding his garden. Stepping out with him, I planned to meet Meranda down by the stream.

"Going to see the girl again, eh?"

"Yes," I said, "unless you'll be needing me?"

"No, go on lad, but I'd watch out if I were you, she can only bring trouble or heartache. I'd be careful of her father too. No telling what could happen if he ever became suspicious of whom you truly are."

"Don't worry Emery, we're just friends, that's all." I turned away from the old man and headed upstream.

"Come on Jiggers!" I called, and the old hound followed me along the trail.

I had told Emery not to worry, but there was reason to be worried. Meranda and I had been getting closer to each other than her father approved. If he ever found out who I really was he'd have no hesitation in turning me over to the county steward and being rid of me. Still, he had no clue of who I actually was and he had no way of finding out.

As I made my way to the fishing hole, I thought of Meranda. She was the only girl I had ever told my feelings too without first having numbed myself with ale. I truly loved her. She was wonderful and understanding and she liked me for who I was. I only wished I could tell her who I really was.

The day was getting quite warm when I reached the shallow part of the stream where I waded across. Jiggers had followed me and he loved the water. First he stopped and lapped some up and then he jumped into the current, which covered his body and left only his head sticking out. Grunting and snorting, he crossed the stream and then he stopped to drink again. As he shook himself off, I heard someone giggle behind me. I turned, and there stood Meranda.

"I see you brought Jiggers again."

"You know he loves the water." Greeting her with an affectionate hug, I smelled the perfume she wore and for the instant I embraced her I knew what heaven was like.

"It's good to see you," she whispered with her sweet voice.

"Come, let's hike along the stream." I took her hand in mine and we began to walk. We wandered up the trail beside the flowing water and headed toward the deep forest.

Passing the bluebells and wild flowers, which were in full bloom, we talked and laughed as the forest grew darker. Underneath the canopy of conifers, it was as though we were in a cathedral made of trees. The holes and angles of branches were covered with moss and the air was moist with dew.

We found ourselves a place to rest upon a fallen log and a young deer journeyed past us not more than twenty feet away. We watched silently, enjoying its graceful beauty. Amazingly, even Jiggers sat quietly by. His ears were pricked and his nostrils flared with each quick whiff of air he inhaled, but still he did not bark or give chase.

Seeing the young deer brought back the memory of the fawn that had entered the grove of trees when I was near death several months before. I could picture the animal licking my forehead as if to comfort me, but still I wasn't sure whether the whole experience had been a dream or not.

As Meranda's eyes followed the deer, I gazed upon her lovely face. I immensely wanted to tell her who I really was and all that had happened to me in the past months. My lips began to move and I almost spoke, but something held me back. Someday, I thought, after avenging my father, I shall tell her.

A few moments later, after watching the deer amble off into the woods, we started back. As we walked, Meranda suddenly spoke in a tone that I knew was about to deliver bad news. "Jacob, I don't really know how to say this, but I'm afraid I have to."

I stopped and turned to her and took her hands in mine. "What—what is it?"

She would not look at me but kept her eyes on the ground. "I don't know if we should see each other any more."

"Why not?" I questioned, as my stomach suddenly became nauseous. "What did I do? Did I do something wrong?"

She pulled her hands away from me and twisted them together, but still she wouldn't look me in the eye. "No, you haven't done anything wrong, but—"

"But what? I thought you cared for me! I thought we were more than friends!"

"We are!" she cried, beginning to sob, "but I don't think anything can come from this! You know our relationship will never lead to marriage. It's just a waste of our time pretending. My father will choose a wealthier man for me and I must be happy with that. It only hurts my heart to see you so much. You're a peasant like me, but you are poorer and own no land. My father would never allow us to be more than friends. He's already thinking of reasons for me not to see you." Meranda wiped her eyes and turned away weeping.

My heart sank in my chest and despair swept over me, but in the far corners of my mind I knew what she said was right. I had just hoped that if we never talked about it, we'd never have to face it, but the truth was now confronting us. I didn't know what to say to her. Hoping to find an answer, I grabbed her shoulders and turned her toward me to search her soft blue eyes, but she spun away from me.

"I love you Meranda!" I cried.

She stopped, turned around and softly kissed my lips. Then, before I knew it, she was scurrying down the path away from me.

I collapsed to the ground and there I rested. Picking up a handful of dirt, I angrily threw it down. She was right and I knew it, but that didn't make me feel any better. I loved her more than anything in the world. "Why?" I bellowed. "Why does this have to happen to me?" I rolled on to my back and the tears came. Jiggers nestled next to me whimpering. Maybe my feelings were too strong, but for years I'd hidden them with drink, and I wasn't quite sure how to deal with them yet. Each day seemed to bring a whole new adventure in emotions for me. It was grand when I felt good, but it could be hell when I felt alone, and at that moment I was alone.

It was dusk by the time I got myself up and headed back to the old man's cabin. A few gray clouds gathered in the pink glow of the western sky, but not enough to bring a drop of rain.

As I ambled home, I began focusing my thoughts on the imminent future and determined that I had been wasting my time. My father's murderer was now my mother's husband, and what had I been doing? —Falling in love with a peasant girl! I felt ashamed of myself and, as I trudged through the bracken and bramble of the dim forest, I resolved to spend all my time practicing the skills that Emery was teaching me. And soon, when I was ready, I would kill Cyrus Everett.

By the time I reached the cabin, the old man was already laying on his mattress. "There's bread and bacon for you lad. Eat up and get some sleep."

I walked over to the small table in the corner and picked up a piece of bread. It was stale and hard. I tossed it back down and began to undress.

"I need you to go into town tomorrow. We're nearly out of salt and I've still a pot of honey you can trade."

"Okay," I said, "but keep your honey. I've got plenty of coin and you've done too much for me already. I'll get the salt and buy some cheese too."

"Don't buy too much, nor let anyone know how much money you have. A wealthy peasant brings on suspicion or worse yet, unseen eyes may wait for you in the forest on your return."

"I'll be careful," I replied, thinking that the old man worried too much. Sitting down, I picked up the bread again and decided to eat it. Afterwards I lay on my bed, and with a heavy heart I slept.

When I awoke, Emery was still sleeping. I threw some wood onto the glowing coals in the hearth and hastened down to the stream to wash my face and hands. The morning was chilly and a number of clouds lingered low in the sky. After quickly washing, I hurried back inside and ate some stale bread chasing it down with a horn of fresh water. The fire had now sprung to life again and I enjoyed its friendly warmth for a moment, subsequently I was ready for my trek to Cawston.

"Emery," I spoke, nudging him by the shoulders. "Emery, I'm going now. Is there anything else you want besides the salt?"

"No my lad. That should do it. Now let an old man sleep!" He rolled over and covered his head with his blanket.

Before leaving the cabin, I opened the door and peered outside. The clouds were growing thick, so I grabbed an old wool hood of Emery's to take along in case it rained on my way to town. Then I stepped out into the cool morning air and began my trek at a brisk pace.

Cawston was northeast, roughly six or seven miles away. Its existence relied mostly on being a crossroad for travelers who journeyed between the nearby towns of Sprowston, Aylsham, and my own village of Dereham. Like any simple village it had its own church, blacksmith, baker, miller, and brewer. Near the center of town was the main keep where the Lord, his family, and his servants lived.

It took me three hours to travel the winding and not so obvious path that led through the forest. The trail was muddy with fallen logs and branches hindering my way, but by late morning I was strolling past the fields on the outskirts of town.

Once I entered the village, I quickly found a spice peddler willing to sell me some salt. It cost me eight pennies for a pound. A high price, but he was likely the only man in town who sold spices. Anyway, I wanted to get my business over with as quickly as possible since it was an onerous hike back and the sky was continually growing darker.

On the way to the dairy I passed the village brewers, which was distinctly marked by a fir branch tied above the door. Stopping for a moment, I scoffed at it, thinking how I no longer needed drink to give me strength and confidence. It controlled me no more, I thought. Then I continued on my way to the dairy to buy some cheese.

*   *   *

I frowned as I stared into the thick dark brew in front of me, my hand wrapped around the warm mug. The friendly glow that had undulated from my stomach to my head had disappeared after my second glass. Only a senseless insatiable craving guided the ale to my lips now.

I glanced over to the corner of the room where a lanky man with a prominent protruding nose was seated. I was sure he was watching me and I thought I recognized him, but from where? I wondered.

It didn't matter. What did matter was that I'd broken my promise to myself. After I had gone to the dairy and procured some cheese, I had passed the tavern again. Something, maybe self-pity over losing Meranda, had drawn me inside. And now I hated myself for it.

Here I am, quaffing again—and what is it doing for me? I'm certainly not enjoying myself, yet still I bring the ale to my lips and drink! What evil have I done to deserve this?

The day went on and the ale poured. The tavern was filled with men, mostly craftsmen and travelers, enjoying a bit of drink and conversation. A great crackling fire burned in the center of the room and smoke twirled up toward the open hole in the roof.

By mid-afternoon I was stumbling drunk and my thoughts were becoming chaotic. I glanced again at the lanky man in the corner. This time he was talking with two other men who were seated at the table with him. Their backs were to me. He gestured in my direction with his eyes and his companions turned around to look. When they found me gazing at them they quickly diverted their eyes elsewhere. Their faces appeared familiar to me also and I was sure I had seen them before. In my foolish drunkenness I stood up and stumbled over to them.

"What are you looking at?" I roared. "Do you have a dispute with me?"

The lean man with the prominent nose stared at me for a moment and then he turned toward the two other men. "What do you think?" he asked.

"It looks like him," replied one of the men whose thick red hair curled down around his muscular shoulders.

"He does indeed," spoke the other man with a belly that hung over his breeches. "A dash rough and grubby, but he does bear a resemblance."

"Hey! I'm speaking to you!" I pointed my finger at the slim man, nearly touching his carrot of a nose.

He continued to ignore me and took an annoying sip from his mug. Then he spoke. "More than a resemblance, I should think."

"But it can't be him," replied the red haired man, "he's dead."

"Remember though," retorted the lanky man with his immense nostrils flaring, "they never found his body when they went back for it. Only Hector's was found at the scene."

"Ah, don't tell me you two think he's still alive," chided the chubby man after taking a swallow of ale. "The foxes ate his body. Hector's corpse was half devoured when they found it."

In my drunkenness I hadn't an inkling of what they were talking about. If I had, I would've left the tavern as fast as I could, but instead my anger grew and I shouted. "Damn you! I'm speaking to you!"

Finally, the men glared at me and laughed. My blood boiled. I reached for my sword and began to withdraw it, but before it was halfway out of its scabbard, the trio was upon me. They threw me up against the wall and the thin wiry man punched me in the gut with a driving blow.

"What's your discord, lad?" I heard one of them say as I was struck across the face with a blunt object. Blood oozed from my mouth and a sharp pain raced through my jaw.

For the next few moments, I felt only punches up and down my body and then I was thrown to the ground and kicked repeatedly. I rolled up into a ball to protect myself. Then I heard a voice. It was the brewer.

"All right you hooligans! You've played enough for one day!" he thundered as he stepped toward us. The brewer was a gigantic bull of a man with huge powerful hands. "Can't you ruffians find a fairer fight than three on one or do you want me to join the lad's side?"

The kicks and punches began to subside and the three men backed away.

"Go on, out with you!" shouted the brewer.

The trio headed toward the door and the lean man yelled, "You've not seen the last of us, lad!"

As they stepped out, I heard the muffled voice of the red haired man speaking to the other two, "Cyrus would pay us at least a shilling—"

His voice faded and I couldn't hear the rest, but it was enough to start the wheels spinning in my head. A dreadful feeling came over me as I realized the magnitude of what I had just heard. If Cyrus was informed that I might still be alive, then any advantage I had was now gone. How stupid could I have been?

"Are you okay, son?" The brewer asked, as his mammoth hands reached down and lifted me off of the earthen floor.

I didn't answer him. My body winced with pain and as I tried to stand, I felt queasy. My head started spinning and a colorful array of spots began forming before my eyes. The last event I recall of that evening was seeing the dismayed expression on the face of the brewer as my vomit ran down his shirt.

*   *   *

When I awoke, my body ached from head to toe. I lay next to a hearth on a paltry pile of straw in what I presumed was still the tavern. Above me, shone a light through a hole in the thatched roof, and though my mind was still muddled from the prior evenings debauchery, I realized that it was a new day. I peered around the dark smoky room and saw that I was alone except for the brewer who slept in the corner on a mat. Slowly and quietly I stood so as not to wake the man.

Upon standing, everything in the room began twirling about me and my vision grew dim. I quickly sat down to let the wave of dizziness pass over me. The brewer rolled over on his mat and smacked his lips. I remained silently by, staring at him, and hoping he wouldn't wake. If he woke, I knew he would ask me many questions, which at that moment, I didn't have time to answer. I needed to get out of Cawston in case Cyrus got word of what had happened the night before and came searching for me.

I took a deep breath and stood. Again I felt dizzy, but I forced myself to go on and staggered to the door. When I opened it the light of day hit me like a mallet, nearly knocking me over, but I pressed on one step at a time.

It was just after sunrise and the muddy streets of town were still empty. With any luck, I'd be out of Cawston in minutes and on my way back to Emery's. If I was really fortunate, the rogues I had met the prior evening hadn't truly cared at all about who I really was. Hopefully they had just been looking for a reason to brawl.

As I ambled along, I opened my handbag. My money was still in it, and so was the salt. I couldn't recall what had happened to the cheese I had bought, but I didn't care. I just wanted to get back to the old man's cabin.

Soon, and without difficulty, I was out of the village. As I trudged forth on the path that led homeward, my head pounded like a blacksmith's hammer. What kind of fool was I? I wondered. I believed I had control of myself, but when the chance of a sip of ale came before me, I fell like a slain beast. Could I ever stay away from the drink or would this malady afflict me forever? My hands trembled and beads of sweat oozed from my skin. What's wrong with me? God, why do I deserve such anguish?

Finally, after a few hours of self-torment, which seemed like days, I reached the stream that flowed adjacent to the old man's cabin. Another half mile and I'd be there. I bent down on my knees and reached out into the water with my hands. Cupping the cool, clear liquid, I brought it to my lips and drank. Then I laid down on the green grass to rest for a moment and gazed up at the sky.

There were a number of clouds scattered hither and thither like strokes of a brush on a canvas of deep blue. The sky appeared so peaceful and welcoming that I wanted to stay there forever until it consumed me and all my troubles. It didn't, so I stood and began hiking the rest of the way home.

As I plodded along the path, I noticed that the effects of the prior night's drinking binge were starting to subside and I was beginning to feel a bit better. My body and especially my jaw were still sore from the scuffle, but my head didn't feel so wretched as it had earlier in the morning.

Maybe I'm not in such a terrible mess, I reasoned. After all, I haven't seen any of Cyrus' men searching for me. Maybe the rogues I'd met last night were just baiting me for their own amusement. That was probably it. I shouldn't be so worried I told myself and I began walking with a lighter step.

Minutes later, Emery's cabin was in view and it appeared remarkably serene and tranquil there beside the stream. It really wasn't a bad place to reside and I wondered why more people didn't live out in the forest away from the towns and villages. Maybe I'll build an estate in such a place someday, I thought.

When I was almost to the door of the cabin, I glanced down and saw hoof prints covering the muddy earth. For a second, my mind couldn't grasp the meaning of it, but then a wave of panic shot through my soul and I rushed into the cabin. The first thing I saw was Emery's bed turned over and my old clothes were glaringly displayed. The old man's few possessions had been smashed upon the floor and lying next to the remnants were two bloodied men unbeknownst to me. The cabin smelled of death and there were puddles of crimson slowly seeping into the earth all around. Nausea overcame me and I wretched.

"Emery! Emery! Where are you?" I shouted, coughing on my vomit. There was no answer. My hands trembling, I swallowed hard and yelled again. "Emery! Emery!" Standing silent for a moment, I listened. I heard a soft noise behind me, so I turned and rushed over to the corner of the room.

There on the earthen floor, under a broken stool, laid Emery. Beside him was a widespread pool of blood and his abdomen was but one extensive open wound. I bent down near his face and breath still flowed from his lips. I sat on the floor next to him as tears came to my eyes. Then I lifted his head and set it in my lap. Emery's eyes opened. I didn't know what to say.

"Cyrus and his men—you must go Winston." He uttered, in barely an audible voice.

"No, I won't leave you here! You'll be okay!" I stroked my fingers through his thin gray hair. "I'll make some medicine, you'll be alright!"

"There is no medicine that can help me now. Go and save yourself. Someday, you can avenge your father's murder and mine too."

"No, no, no, I won't let you die!" I protested with tears pouring from my eyes.

"Don't be afraid, I am not. Look around—do you see the stains of blood? Do you see the dead?"

I gazed around the room and again saw the puddles of blood and the two slain men.

"The blood is not all mine," whispered Emery with a twinkle in his deep blue eyes.

I tried to smile, though I could hardly bear the sight of him in such a wretched state. I knew that the old man had fought bravely and I understood that he was pleased with himself for that.

"There were five including Cyrus," he rasped, before struggling fiercely for another breath. "I killed two and wounded the rest. They left me here for dead and went back to Dereham—but they'll return."

"You did good," I said trembling, wishing I could say something more to comfort him. "You did real good."

He gave me his hand and I held firmly on to it. "Now you must go," he gasped, "take care, my friend."

"I will," I replied, massaging his worn wrinkled hand. A moment later it was limp and a bone chilling draft wafted over me. I rested there for a few minutes with Emery's head in my lap and caressed his pale cheeks. Then, as my tears flowed, I closed his eyes and laid his head back down on the hard earth.

In the stillness of the cabin, my ears detected a low muffled noise. It was soft and in the distance, but it was slowly becoming louder. Suddenly I realized what it was. It was the sound of a horse galloping.

No, it was more than one horse—it was at least two or three. It had to be more of Cyrus' men returning to search for me.

I quickly glanced around the cabin for anything I might need. My eyes found the old man's sword lying next to his lifeless body. I grabbed it and dashed out through the door.

The sound from the galloping horses grew louder and I knew at any moment I might see the riders coming out of the forest. I took to my heels, racing around the cabin and down to the stream. From there I scrambled up the path along the waterway toward the old man's fishing hole. I continued until the wind tore at my lungs and I could run no more. When I stopped, my chest heaved with each gasp of air and sweat poured down my face. I began to walk, turning around every few seconds to be sure that no one was following me.

Soon, I reached the fishing hole and I stopped to rest and clear my head. I didn't know what to do or where to go. There was no one I could trust except for Meranda, and the fishing hole was the only place I might find her without being seen by anyone else. I hid myself in the thicket bordering the stream incase Cyrus' men came searching for me. I had no idea whether Meranda would come down to the stream that day or even the next, but I knew of nothing else I could do. Forlorn, exhausted, and laden with a heavy heart, I waited.

CHAPTER FIVE

It was evening when Meranda emerged from the trail that led from her home and walked along the bank of the stream. She appeared distraught and seemed to be searching for someone. Who? I wondered. Could it be me? Maybe, but just two days ago she had told me she didn't want to see me anymore. Why would she be seeking me, unless she knew something had happened? Did she know something about Emery's death?

I gazed up the trail from where she had come. No one followed her, so I stepped out from behind the brush and waded across the stream.

"Jacob! Or should I say Winston?" She glared at me with contempt, but also with relief. "You're okay?"

"Yes, I'm fine," I replied, accepting the fact that she now knew who I really was.

"A man from Dereham came by my father's home this morning on his way to Cawston," she said, her cheeks flushed a brilliant red. "He and his men were looking for Winston Tabor! His name was Everett."

"You didn't tell him about me, did you?" I asked.

"No!" She shook her head and tears came to her eyes. "I said nothing, though I suspected it was you, especially after the man described what he—you looked like!"

"Then how? How did he know where to go?" I grabbed Meranda by her shoulders and shook her. "He killed Emery!"

"My father," she cried, "it was my father!"

Meranda turned away weeping and I realized I was taking out my rage for Emery's death on her. "I'm sorry, I didn't mean to yell or hurt you."

"You're sorry?" she sobbed. "Is that all you can say, after lying to me about who you are and what you've done?" She brushed her hair from her face and wiped her eyes. "I loved you!"

"I wanted to tell you but—"

"You wanted to tell me how you murdered your own father, but you couldn't find a delicate way to put it? Is that it? Or did you think we could just keep playing this charade forever?"

"I never killed my father! On my word, I swear to you, I never did that! It was Everett who killed him and he almost killed me too! He lies like a snake and that's how he convinced my mother to marry him! It was all a plan so he could become Lord of Dereham!"

"And I should believe you? I should believe the word of a fugitive? Oh, it doesn't matter! I came here only to be sure you were still alive! What good it has done, I don't know?"

"Meranda, you've got to believe me!" I reached out for her and she withdrew.

"See me no more, Winston! I'll tell no one I saw you, but leave me be!" She turned and hurried up the path away from the stream.

"Meranda! Meranda!" I called out, but she paid no heed. I watched as her graceful figure dashed up the trail and disappeared behind the brush. While taking in the last glimpse of her, a wave of grief washed over me. I didn't know if I'd ever see her again.

I stood there vexed for a moment, not knowing what to do and feeling sorry for myself. I was completely alone, but I had not the luxury to waste my time in a quagmire of self-pity. Quickly I thought of what I must do to survive. My only hope would be to stay out of sight of Cyrus and his men and to try and find my good friend Eric. He would surely help me.

Eric had lived at my father's manor when I was a child. At the age of seven he had been sent by his father, Lord Braden, to begin his training as a knight. First as a page and then as a squire to my father, our family grew to love him. He was like a brother to me and a son to my parents. It was only a year ago that he had been knighted in ceremony and had left for London to engage in business for his father.

London, I decided, was where I would go.

*   *   *

Two days passed quickly on my journey to London. I had traveled at night and slept in the brush by the side of the highway during the day. I had seen no sign of Cyrus or his men along the road, and with that in mind, my cautiousness began to wane as my hunger increased.

I had discarded the old sword I'd been using and in its sheath I placed the elaborate blade of Emery's that I had retrieved from the cabin. To hide the detailed hilt of the sword, I tore a piece of wool from my tunic and tied it around it. In that way, no one could see what a fine blade I carried and no questions would be asked about it.

On my third day of travel, I came to the small town of Haverhill and stopped for a bit of food. I bought a loaf of bread, which I quickly consumed, at the small bakery. Then I bought a few strips of salted pork from the butcher. Sadness came over me as I passed the only tavern in the village. It reminded me of my failure to control my want for ale.

If only I hadn't drank again, I thought, Emery would still be alive and we'd be laughing and joking, resting by the fire in his old cottage. Instead, Emery was gone forever and there was nothing I could do to bring him back. Why had I broken my promise to myself?

While reflecting on my failures, I came upon a stone bridge. The span covered a shallow waterway that was quite foul. It was the runoff from the dirty streets of Haverhill. Why it occurred to me then and there, I'll never know, but as I gazed into the dark smelly water below, I realized I could never promise myself that I would not indulge in ale again. I had learned that my own promises were too easily broken. I could only try my hardest to stay sober each day, as it came, not worrying about the next. I recognized that what I had was a malady and it couldn't be cured in a week or a month, not even a year. As the old man had told me, it would be a life long struggle. I stared into the black dingy water below and spat. My spit landed with a slap on the surface and there it stayed, like the dolor in my heart, with no current to wash it away.

Eventually, I was able to pull away from my disconcerted thoughts and I continued on over the bridge. As I passed the last few cottages of the village, I took out a bit of salted pork from my wallet and slowly nibbled on it. It wasn't the freshest of meat and at that moment I really wasn't hungry, but I forced myself to eat. I knew I needed the nourishment if I was going to stay strong and healthy enough to eventually confront Cyrus.

Ahead of me the highway twisted and turned through a lavish green meadow and I followed it, for that was the way to London. The road itself was in bad condition after the months of winter frost and the hard rains of spring. There were abundant ruts and potholes and a myriad of puddles, some of which were at least two feet deep. A wagon or cart would have had a tough go and even a man on horseback would have needed to employ caution.

After an hour or so the road twisted into a thick green forest. Above the tall trees the sun's warm rays shone down through the branches and speckled the forest floor with patches of light. I was getting warm and a bit thirsty, so I was delighted when I heard the babbling of a gentle brook. The brook flowed toward the road, came to a bend, and then led away from it. I stepped off of the path and into the brush where the water came nearest to the road.

Kneeling down, I leaned out over the current and used my hands to drink. Then, holding my breath, I dipped my whole head into the brook and enjoyed the chilling sensation it delivered to my skin. I washed my face and then flung my head back. The cool water from my hair dripped inside my tunic and between my shoulders. It felt splendid. After resting alongside the brook for a few minutes, I was on my way again with a light breeze whipping at my back.

The road quickly led me into an even deeper forest and I saw what appeared to be someone sitting or squatting over the highway. After a number of yards further, I found that my summation was correct. There was a man resting on the ground and he appeared to be in distress. I raced up to him and he was holding his knee in anguish.

He was an aged man with a bulbous ruddy nose and a glowing face. He wore wool breeches, a shirt, and a tunic, which were worn and obviously very old. A few teeth were missing from his broad lipped mouth and his hair was a ragged curly red. He appeared to be a beggar or tramp.

He motioned with his arm for me to come closer. "It's a good thing you wandered by my boy. No telling how long I'd have waited for anyone else to come along this ill-used highway."

"Are you alright?" I questioned. "What's wrong with your knee?"

"Oh, I don't know. Seems I can't straighten it out all the way. I was walking and it just collapsed on me. What can a poor old soul do?"

"I'm not sure, but I'll help you stand." I leaned over to grab his left arm and shoulder when I saw a movement in the underbrush. At the same time I noticed the tramp's right hand was hidden under his tunic. A dreadful feeling came over me and I realized the whole display was a set up. I was about to be robbed.

Before I had time to think, the knave pulled out a dagger and swung it toward my chest. Instinctively I stepped back and before I knew it, my sword was out of its scabbard and in my hands. I swung it down fast on the tramp's outstretched arm and, being sharper than I could have imagined, my blade sliced through his wrist with barely a sound. His hand, with the knife still in it, dropped to the ground and blood squirted from his stub in rhythmic spurts.

I watched the tramp's eyes. First he gazed at his severed appendage and then he gaped at me. Never in my whole life had I seen such an expression of surprise and terror in a man's face. His eyes seemed to ask, "Why? How did this happen?" Then he screamed and a horrendous cry filled the air, but I had no time to listen.

From behind me came two men, cohorts of the first I presumed. These men were younger and both yielded swords. The man on my right came at me swinging his blade to my left side. I blocked the blow with my sword and I spun backward to my right. Coming completely around, I swept my blade across his neck.

Dropping his weapon, the rogue placed his hands on his throat. There was a deep gash in his neck and blood surged from the wound in two separate streams. He stumbled backward and a gurgling sound resonated from his throat. He was choking on his own blood.

I turned to face the third man, but he had stepped back and away from me. His eyes were wide and filled with shock and dismay over the sight of his two associates.

I glanced back at the outlaw whose throat was severed. His eyes rolled up in his head and he fell forward to the ground with a thud and a splatter of crimson.

Then, from the corner of my eye, I caught a movement. It was the ruddy old tramp who had lost his hand. He'd gathered himself, picked up his knife in his other hand, and came rushing toward me in a rage. "You'll die in hell for this, you bastard!" he screeched.

I took a stride toward him and plunged my sword, aiming for his heart. I missed and my blade entered his abdomen, exiting through his back. In his madness, the tramp was still able to strike out at me with his knife and he made a fine cut on my right shoulder. I pulled up and down on my sword causing his belly to gash and his entrails spilled out. Crimson poured from his wide-open mouth and his eyes bulged in anguish. His body shook violently for a moment and then, quivering, he fell backward. I pulled out my sword from his lifeless body and readied myself for the next assault.

When I turned to face the third man again, he was gone. I peered down the road in the direction I had come and caught a glimpse of him running away. I was relieved.

Reaching down to wipe the blood from my sword onto the dead tramps clothes, I took a deep breath and wiped the sweat from my brow. It had all happened so fast. Fortunately, I had learned more from Emery than I had presumed.

"Magnificent! That was superb!" came a voice, seemingly from nowhere.

I glanced around to see who it was. From out of the brush sauntered a chubby middle-aged man with a round face and light curly hair. His lips were full and his cheeks were flushed and he was clapping his hands together. The clothes he wore appeared to be the kind a gentleman might wear, but they were worn, wrinkled, and dirty.

"Great show, my lad!"

"Who are you?" I questioned. "Why were you hiding?" Then, thinking that the fellow might be part of the party who had just tried to rob me, I backed up quickly and readied my sword. "If you're a highwayman you'd better step back or I shall do to you what I've done to these men." I gestured with my left hand toward the two lifeless bodies that rested in the dirt.

Waving his hands back and forth and chuckling, he said, "No my boy, you've got it wrong! I'm no outlaw; I'm but a simple peddler. I came upon you and those men while you were fighting. Not knowing at first who would win, naturally I hid myself in the brush."

"Ah, a coward." I said.

"Call me what you will, but I haven't lived this long by sticking my neck out where it doesn't belong. Besides, I've no sword, not even a knife. What help would I have been, but in your way?"

"I suppose you're right, but bravery certainly doesn't flow in your blood."

"Bravery is often confused with foolishness," he replied.

"I guess you could make a valid argument with that."

"Good, then we can be friends?"

I nodded and extended my hand out to greet him. "My name's Winston," I said, using my real name, for I was tired of lying to people about who I really was.

"I'm Donovan."

We shook hands and I said, "Help me take these bodies into the brush. I'd not like to explain to the county steward why these men are laying here."

"I understand completely. Anyway, I owe you a favor. If you'd not come along and ruined these men's livelihood, I'd have been their next victim."

Donovan bent down and rummaged through the pockets of the two dead men and inspected their handbags for anything of value. "You sure made a mess of them, that you did. Did you have to cut off the old bloke's hand and spill his guts?"

"Come on," I said. "Are you going to help or are you going to babble?"

"Okay, okay, what's your hurry? Can't a good fellow make a little conversation?"

I didn't answer him.

"Look!" rang Donovan's voice again as he held up one of his hands. "Look what I found! Two shillings and four pennies, more money than you've likely seen at any one time."

I gave the peddler a stern glance.

"Course, half of it's yours," he muttered quickly.

"Keep your money, just help me get these bodies off of the road!"

"If that's the way you want it, fine!" He opened his wallet and placed the money inside. Then he reached down and picked up the knife that had nearly been the death of me. "Not a bad dagger either," he muttered, placing the knife in his wallet also.

We carried each corpse into the undergrowth of the forest and tossed ivy and fallen branches on top of them. By the time we were done, it was late afternoon and the sun would be setting in a few hours. I wanted to get moving so I could find a good place, near fresh water, to sleep for the night.

It turned out that Donovan was headed for London too, so it appeared that I had a traveling partner whether I wanted one or not. As we walked along the road, we talked about nothing in particular. Actually, Donovan did most of the talking and I did the listening. I learned that he was a peddler of most anything and everything. He was going to London to buy colored silk and wools, or anything else that might sell for a handsome profit in a modest village.

I knew his type. They wandered from town to town selling their wares while telling hard luck stories to the kind-hearted for free handouts. They, like him, meant no harm. They just made a living the only way they knew how. And now it appeared that I was stuck with him, at least for a while.

*   *   *

Two days later, Donovan and I were still traveling together. He was a happy-go-lucky sort of fellow and although he talked too much, he was genuinely friendly and he began to grow on me. Along the way, he told me about his schemes to become a rich man and all the wonderful things he'd do with his wealth. It was obvious to me, and maybe even to him, that he would have been rich long ago if his schemes had actually ever worked. He was merely daydreaming out loud, but it was a way to stay optimistic and make it through another day.

What Donovan lacked in material possessions, he certainly made up for in spirit. He simply enjoyed living and that's all that really mattered to him. I had known many a nobleman who was rich in power and wealth, but none had as much love of life as did the plump jolly fellow I was traveling with.

It was late afternoon and we were a few miles outside of Hertford when we stopped for the night just off of the highway. We planned on passing through Hertford the next day and from there London would only be a days journey away.

We found a narrow grassy clearing adjacent to a creek that was surrounded by oak trees and brush. The sky was clear and the air was warm, making it a good place for us to rest for the night. I had bought some meat and bread earlier in the day in Bury, so we sat down to eat before preparing our beds for the night.

"Good food!" exclaimed Donovan, tearing off a piece of meat with his teeth from a slab of salted pork. As he gnawed on the flesh, he withdrew a wineskin from his soiled tunic and took a long pull off of it. "Thanks to those gracious gentlemen you met a couple days ago, I was able to buy this today." After he spoke, Donovan laughed and a few chunks of meat and saliva flew from his mouth. Next, he gestured for me to take the wineskin.

"No," I said.

"What? Not thirsty?"

"No, I don't partake in drink."

"Ah, so you're a drinkwater." He shrugged his shoulders and took another swig from the bag. "That's okay by me, all the more wine for myself."

Leaning back on my elbow, I gazed at Donovan and shook my head. "You silly man."

"Silly yes, but foolish never," he replied and a smile broke on his face. We both laughed.

"I'm going to get a drink down at the creek," I said as I stood.

Donovan nodded as he picked a large chunk of meat from his teeth with his fingers.

After taking a few steps toward the water, I remembered I wanted to shave, so I turned around to retrieve my wallet. When I reached down to pick up the handbag that contained my razor blade, the old peddler gazed at me.

"Oh, so you don't trust me, eh?" he said with a disappointing expression on his flushed face.

"No, it's not that, I just needed my razor blade."

"You don't have to make up excuses. Though you should trust a man who actually carries a piece of the cross that our Lord Jesus Christ died on."

I glared at him strangely and wondered what rubbish would spew from his lips next.

The fleshy man reached his hand down into a pocket of his breeches and pulled out three tiny pieces of wood. "Here!" he exclaimed as he held out a sliver of wood in his hand. "This is the real thing. With this you can heal the sick and cure the blind. It's from the very cross that our Savior was crucified on. I hold a fragment right here in my hand. I have three myself but only one is needed to make miracles happen, so for you my friend, for a small price, I shall part with one of them."

"Ha!" I barked. "If I didn't know you, I'd cut out your tongue! Save your speeches for the feeble-witted!" I turned and headed for the creek.

Behind me I heard Donovan laugh and mutter, "Unbeliever."

I shook my head in frustration, but I couldn't help but smile. What a silly man, I thought.

A moment later I was at the creek that was only a stone's throw away from our campsite. I bent down and reached out into the cool fresh water and brought it to my lips. Glancing up, I noticed a small pool alongside the creek where the water was clear and quiet. Since the day had been warm and the evening was still quite nice, I decided to bathe myself.

I took off my sword and belt of rope, pulled off my tunic, leather shoes, stockings, and breeches and then stepped into the soothing liquid. The bottom of the pool was sandy and soft on my feet. I squatted and laid back in the pleasant calm water. It had been at least two weeks since I'd last bathed in the stream near Emery's cabin and after all that had happened to me since, I really needed to wash.

The sun was nearly over the hills far to the west and the sky shone a brilliant pink. I scrubbed my body with sand and worked my sore muscles with my hands. Then I rested silently in the comforting pool, listening to the birds and the gentle flow of the creek.

Gazing down at the still surface of the water, I noticed my reflection in the fading light. It had been many months since I'd seen my own face and the last time had been in a mirror at my father's castle.

I appeared different now. No more did my face show the pudginess of an easy life filled with drinking and feasting. My features were thin and coarse and my wavy brown hair was much longer than it had ever been. My dark eyes, which peered out from behind high cheekbones, reflected back at me with a haunting stare. Glancing at my arms and legs, I noticed they were tight and fibrous and I could see each muscle twitch under my skin when I moved. I had changed so much that my appearance startled me. I resembled a man much more than I actually felt I was. Surely I wasn't the same boy who had been left to die in that lonely grove of trees over seven months before. Was I?

My changed appearance would certainly help me avoid anyone from recognizing me. I wondered how the three men in the tavern in Cawston had recognized me so easily. Of course, with a mug of ale in my hand, it probably gave them a good clue as to who I really was.

After shaving, I watched the pink light over the horizon slowly fade away. Then I stood and squeezed the water from my hair. I stepped out of the pool feeling quite refreshed and tore a strip of cloth from my tunic to tie my hair back. I regretted putting on the same clothes, for they were old and pungently offensive, but I had nothing else to wear.

When I traipsed back to the campsite for the evening, Donovan was already asleep and snoring loudly. I laid myself down on the grassy earth and stared up at the stars. Within minutes, I too was asleep.

CHAPTER SIX

The sky was clear and the sun was just rising when Donovan and I awoke. There was a slight chill in the air and the grass was wet with morning dew.

I stood yawning and stretched my body up over the tall underbrush. Gazing out past our grassy campsite and toward the fields of oat and hay, I saw that the local peasants were already up and working. Most of them were clearing weeds and thistles that grew between their crops. Others were moving their livestock out to graze the wild assart land.

As I wiped the sleep from my eyes, I wondered what kept those people going. They worked so hard, yet gained so little for what they did. They sweated their lives away so that a chosen few could live in overindulgence. Many of them were serfs and belonged, like material possessions, to their masters. Their only chance of freedom was to hope their lord might someday be kind enough to grant them liberty. Or, if they were brave enough, they could run away to another town for a year and a day and, if they weren't caught by then, they would be free. If they were caught, then only God could help them.

"A poor lot they are, aren't they?" Donovan asked, as if reading my mind.

"Yes, yes they are," I replied, and then as an after thought I muttered, "I can't understand why God lets this be."

"What do you mean?"

"You know, all the pain and suffering in this world. What good does it do? Why does he do this?"

"He doesn't do anything," said Donovan after expelling a long drawn out yawn, "man, in his greed, causes the pain you speak of, not God."

"I suppose that's true, but why does he let it happen? Why doesn't he make men live together peacefully and share freely amongst themselves?" I asked this question merely thinking out loud not really expecting an answer, at least not an answer worth any merit.

"If he did that, then he'd control our souls and we'd never truly be free," replied Donovan. "A man's most happiest and can only find the

Kingdom of Heaven if it's he himself who chooses the right way, not God or anyone else. Some do choose the right way, but many are lazy or greedy. Those are the ones who cause the pain and suffering."

I thought for a moment as I looked out at the toiling peasants and then I examined Donovan inquisitively. "How do you know so much?"

Donovan grinned widely. "I'm mostly foolish," he replied, "but over the years I've picked up a bit of wisdom. Now come on, no more talk of such sadness. Let's have something to eat."

A moment later, we were chewing on the rest of the meat and bread I had bought the day before and soon we were again on our way to London. We traveled fairly fast for men on foot and by noon we were in the town of Hertford.

Hertford was immense compared to my own village of Dereham. It must have contained at least three bakeries, for the smell of fresh bread was everywhere. The streets were crowded with the bustling of merchants selling linens, leathers, fish, wine, and everything else that brought money to the purses of their owners. Since late spring and early summer had been uncommonly warm, the fields had already produced a number of grains and vegetables that were being sold at the many shops. This bountiful early harvest was noticeable in the happy faces and friendly hellos of the townsfolk.

Donovan wanted to go to the nearest tavern but I refused, so we decided to separate for a while. I told him I would meet him back at the alehouse in a couple of hours and we'd continue on our way. He agreed.

With a couple of hours to spend alone, I soon found myself in the market place and I stopped at one of the stalls where a leatherer plied his trade. For five pennies I had the craftsman sew a leather cover, which would not be easily removed, around the hilt of my sword.

"I've no idea why you'd want to cover up something as beautiful as this, unless it's stolen?" said the craftsman with a raised eyebrow.

"It's not stolen, but I'd like to keep it from being stolen from me." I replied to the plump hairy man.

"Never seen nothing like it in my life. Sure like to know where you got it?"

"It was given to me as a gift by someone who was very close."

"Yeah, close as a blade's thrust from you, eh?" he barked satirically, followed by a long hard laugh at his own witless quip.

The idiot was insinuating that I was a thief and a murderer. I felt my blood pulsate in my head and I had a strong urge to skewer the man with my blade. Fortunately, I controlled my rage and forced myself to laugh along with the callow man.

When he was done, I handed him an extra penny and said, "This is for keeping quiet about what you've seen here."

"Seen what?" he asked, followed by another bellowing laugh.

He may be a coarse and stupid man, I thought, but he was a good leather worker. The intricate detail on the hilt of my sword was covered up completely by tough firm leather and when placed in its sheath it looked of nothing but a peasant's sword.

After leaving the market place, I wandered about the town a bit and passed the main keep where the Lord lived. The castle was built on a hill and was quite magnificent with its massive stonewalls and jutting towers. It was much greater than my father's manor and undoubtedly its owner was a very wealthy man. I had only seen such a splendid estate once or twice before in my life.

Continuing on, I investigated the town for a while longer, but soon I felt ready to be on my way again. If I'd been smart, I would have started out by myself without Donovan to slow me down, but I went to meet the middle-aged peddler as I had promised. I proceeded to the alehouse where he had gone and as I came close to it, I heard a ruckus going on. I dashed up to the door and just then, Donovan came out with his arms held behind his back by two large men.

"What's going on?" I questioned.

One of the men with a broad flat nose and thinning hair answered, "This crook here, ate and drank to his fancy and then tried to walk out when the brewer wasn't looking."

"Is that so Donovan?" I asked, giving him a hard glare. "What happened to the money you had?"

"I spent it on wine for my wineskin yesterday," he meekly replied, shrugging his shoulders and gazing at me with a humble expression.

The other man, with lengthy brown curly locks, who was holding Donovan by his left arm growled. "Do you know this con-man?"

I wanted to say, "No, I don't know this man," but I set my eyes upon Donovan again and he contorted his flushed face and fleshy jowls into the expression of a poor helpless puppy.

"Yes, I know this fool and I'm sure I can cover whatever it is he owes you."

"That would be fine," barked the flat nosed man sarcastically, "if he hadn't already committed the crime!"

Then the two men, along with Donovan, pushed by me and began marching down the street. "If you'd like to know, he'll be in the Lord's dungeon till court is held!" shouted one of the men.

I turned and saw the brewer standing in the doorway of the tavern with his arms crossed over his dirty apron and he was smiling. "Serves him right!" he roared. Then he chuckled and turned around, slamming the door behind him.

What was I to do? I had wondered. I could have left for London and been on my merry way, but for some strange reason I felt an allegiance to the foolish peddler. I had to at least find out what the lord of the village would do with him.

As I was standing there on the street, I must have appeared confused, for a tall wiry man with a long pointy nose and shallow dark eyes came up to me. He was dressed elegantly and I presumed he was a merchant.

"You look rather puzzled," he said in a high-pitched voice. "Don't worry though, I saw the whole incident. There's only one thing to do. Uh huh, one thing."

"And what's that?" I asked, wondering if the man truly knew what I should do or if he was playing me as a fool so that he could sell me some worthless article or gadget.

"You must see Lord Stanton if you want your friend to be free again. Yes, uh huh, he's the man to see. He's fair and just. Yes, he will help you."

"Where can I find this Lord Stanton?"

"At the main keep, uh huh, center of town. That's where you'll find him." The awkward man turned his head and stretched out his long arm and pointed toward the magnificent castle I had seen earlier in the day.

As he pointed I glanced at his silhouette. He had an extensive over-bite with broad protruding upper teeth. His protracted nose reminded me of a beak on a bird.

Just then he turned to me. "Are you listening? I said he lives there." He turned again toward the direction of his outstretched hand.

"Yes," I replied with a smile. "I see. Thank you for your help." I reached out my hand and firmly shook his.

He peered at me queerly and finally said, "You're welcome."

I stepped quickly down the street in the direction the gentleman had pointed. The bizarre man had reminded me of the many wandering jesters who had entertained for a meal and a place to stay for the night at my father's court.

Within a few minutes I reached the castle that I had strolled by earlier in the day. The gates were open and with no ongoing feuds or battles at the time, armed guards were not present. I was able to wander right into the courtyard.

A servant, eyeing my dirty clothes, asked me what my business was. I told him of my situation and how I needed to see Lord Stanton in regards to my friend's freedom. He explained that the lord of the manor didn't usually see unannounced visitors, especially peasants, but the servant said he would see what he could do. He motioned me toward a bench and I sat down.

The courtyard was a brilliant site to behold. The main cobblestone walk that led from the outer gates to the main tower was surrounded by a number of neat and tidy diminutive gardens. The gardens were encircled by marble stepping-stones and within each one stood a statue of a saint who seemed to watch over his own limited plot. In the center of the courtyard was a great statue of the Virgin Mary with her hands folded in a position of prayer.

Next to the immense statue sat three young women on a bench dressed in elegant clothing. They were talking and laughing and I presumed they were family or friends of Lord Stanton. One of them, a girl with light blonde hair about my own age, met my eyes for just a second. She flashed a quick smile and then peered away. I smiled back and thought of Meranda and how wonderful it would be to see her again. I pictured her sweet lovely face within my mind and my heart longed for her. Then, remembering where I was, a wave of heat flowed through my cheeks. I was embarrassed.

There I was dressed in filthy clothes and looking like a beggar. What reason did I have to think that a nobleman, a lord in fact, would listen to what I had to say? Thinking that I'd better leave before I had made a total fool of myself, I stood up and began walking toward the gates.

"Just a minute there, I thought you wanted to see me!"

I quickly spun around and there stood a man with long curly locks as black as a raven's. His eyes were dark and intense, yet his face seemed to glow with delight and confidence. I could tell he was an older man, yet he had a youthful appearance about him. His green and red surcoat that displayed his family's coat-of-arms was made of fine linen.

"Why you're just a lad," he said, reaching out his hand to greet me. "I'm Lord Stanton."

I shook his hand and was about to speak, but I'd forgotten what words to say. Though I was born a nobleman, I felt I had no business bothering this important man. I felt especially conscious of myself, being dressed as I was, and standing in the nearby presence of three lovely girls who continued to glance at me and giggle.

"You look bewildered. You're not from around here are you?"

"No," I blurted out, "I'm sorry sir, I didn't mean to bother you. I know you're much too busy for such small matters as mine. I shall leave."

"You shall not!" he insisted, grabbing me by the arm. "I'm not the sort of man to turn a stranger away, be he tramp, beggar, or peasant. If you were from this town you would know that. I try to be gracious and courteous to those I meet unless they show me a reason not to be. Do you understand?"

"I think so."

"Well let me put it another way then, so I know you understand me. Some lords, barons, what have you, govern their domain by making their citizens fear and hate them. I, on the other hand, feel much safer knowing that my subjects respect me and think of me as a friend."

Instantly I thought of my father. That's the way he had ruled over my hometown of Dereham. I had a sudden urge to tell this man that no matter how gracious he was to his people, there was a strong chance that some slithering snake was lying in the grass just waiting for the right moment to strike—a man like Cyrus Everett. I wanted to tell him, but I didn't.

"I'm sorry, what did you say your name was?" he asked.

Though I hadn't yet mentioned my name, I went ahead and told him. "Winston Tabor," I said.

"Winston Tabor, hmm—sounds quite familiar." He placed his right hand to his chin.

Suddenly, I feared I had made a mistake by telling him my real name. Could it be that the lies Cyrus had told had spread this far?

"What is your father's name?"

A bead of sweat immediately formed on my forehead and I wasn't sure how I should answer the man, but I decided to continue telling the truth. "Salem, Salem Taber, but he has passed on now."

"Oh, I'm quite sorry," he said. Then he studied me with his eyes for a moment and crinkled up his brow. "Did your father ever sport in tournament?"

"No," I replied, feeling much relieved by the question he had asked. "He enjoyed watching and I believe he was quite good with a lance, but I never saw him in a tournament."

"Oh well, I guess I was thinking of someone else. No matter. Now, what was it you wished to ask of me?"

"Well," I stammered, "a friend of mine—well actually he's not really my friend—he's a man I met while traveling to London. He seems like a nice fellow and now he's gotten himself in a bit of trouble. I guess I'm here to see if you can help me."

He gazed at me intently with deep searching eyes. "Go on, what's happened to him?"

"To get straight to the point," I said, "he went to a tavern, ate and drank, and then tried to leave without giving compensation."

"Oh, so he's the one who's in my dungeon. You've a kind heart for helping this stranger and I admire a soul who wishes to help others. What is it you ask of me?"

"Nothing really, just let me pay the brewer for the food and drink the old peddler stole and we shall be on our way. I'll even pay a fine if you wish me too."

"And what shall you pay with?"

"I've money in my handbag," I lifted up my wallet with a gesturing motion.

He scrutinized me with his eyes and I knew he was wondering what a peasant, such as I appeared to be, was doing with a purse of coin.

"It's not stolen," I said. "If you're wondering why I'm dressed so poorly, it's because a well dressed man who travels the highway receives much more attention from cut throats and thieves than does a peasant."

"True." He smiled. "You're a smart lad."

"Then you can help?"

"I'm sorry," he replied, "but it's not that easy. In this town, a man must suffer the consequences of his actions. He can't be set free that easily, but maybe there is something that can be done. I've things to attend to now, but if you'll join me for supper, a couple of hours before sundown, then we can talk." Lord Stanton paused for a moment and then furrowed his brow. "You know, you remind me of someone I once knew," he said before shaking my hand firmly and marching off toward the main hall of his castle.

I stood there for a moment pondering the man's intentions. Was he as true as he sounded or was there some dark plot in his mind? Would he really work something out and help me free Donovan? Why couldn't I pay him off like most lords, barons, or earls? Something was different about him and he raised my curiosity. What did he mean when he said I reminded him of someone he once knew? I wasn't sure but I had a feeling I was going to find out.

That afternoon, while waiting for supper, I returned to the market and bought a shirt, tunic, and pair of breeches. I felt I should try to look my best for Lord Stanton that evening. The clothes were made by a peasant woman and, though they were rough and home spun from her own wool, they were clean and fresh. It felt delightful to take off my soiled clothes and replace them with new ones.

That evening, I arrived at the castle around six. Though the common folk usually ate supper earlier, it was stylish for the gentry to eat as late as possible. A servant showed me into the main hall. Resembling other castles, the main hall was used for eating, sleeping for the servants, and almost all activities that needed to be done inside. The floor was made of stone and covered with straw. The walls were made of wood and plaster and great beams of timber held up the roof. In the middle of the floor was an immense stone hearth that contained the fire for warmth and light. The smoke from the crackling fire twirled upward and escaped through a hole in the ceiling. At night, when the day was done, the servants would put away the trestle tables used for eating and playing games upon, and bring out their straw mattresses to sleep on.

At this supper, like most estates, there were three levels of tables arranged for the gathering. The highest one was set for the lord of the manor, his family, and the most noble of guests. The middle table was also for noble, but less important visitors. The lowest table was set for the servants, wandering entertainers, and the rare times when a peasant was invited to dine with his master. Lord Stanton's servant showed me to the lowest table.

I was used to eating in such a great room, being the son of a lord, but I wasn't used to eating at the low table. Seated beside and across from me were two men who greeted me with a nod before continuing on with their conversation. They appeared to be wandering musicians or entertainers. The middle table was occupied by a priest and a number of other guests who paid scant attention to the three of us common citizens.

The smell of cooked meat drifted in from the kitchen and I inhaled deeply to enjoy the wonderful aroma. The man beside me and the one across from me were telling each other stories of their travels and adventures. Being distracted by the servants and their food preparation, I wasn't listening intently on what was being said, but what I did hear sounded like some very tall tales.

Just then, Lord Stanton entered the room wearing the same outfit he had worn earlier in the day. He seated himself at the center of the highest table and appeared to be searching for someone. "Ah, my boy!" he yelled across the room. Everyone glanced up from their conversations to see whom he was speaking too. "Come and sit up here why don't you?" He was gazing at me and waving his arms.

I twisted my head to peer behind me, thinking he must have been speaking to his son or another important youth, but no one else was there.

"You, Winston! Come on up here!"

I stood and meekly ambled up to the table with all eyes upon me.

"I'm glad you could make it. Looks like you got cleaned up or maybe bought yourself some new clothes?"

"Yes sir, I bought some clothes at the market today."

"Good, have a seat." He reached over with his left hand and pulled out a chair.

I was surprised. I'd never before seen a peasant seated at the high table—anywhere. I peered at Lord Stanton and determined that I was going to be the victim of a prank. He's jesting me, I thought. When I sit down, he'll pull the chair out from behind me and everyone will have a good laugh. Well, if it helps to free Donovan, I decided, I will go along with his trick.

I began to sit down, readying myself for the fall, but no fall ever came. The chair stayed where it was and no one was laughing, though a few cold eyes were glued upon me.

Just then the priest, who was wearing an elaborate robe of wool, stood and asked, "Why is it, Lord Stanton, that a peasant dines at the high table while I eat at the middle?"

With a scowl on his face, Lord Stanton answered him with a question. "What was it you preached last Sunday father—something about humbleness?"

The priest returned to his seat grimacing with a wave of red flushing over his cheeks.

Realizing that I truly was welcome to dine at the high table, I showed my appreciation to Lord Stanton. "Thank you sir," I said, "for letting me join you for supper."

"You're very welcome, but don't call me sir. Call me William."

"Thank you William."

"Ah, that's better. Now, before we eat, I'd like you to meet some people."

Now I'll get to meet his family, I thought, and at that moment, seven men strode into the room. Three sat on one side of us and four sat on the other. They all wore surcoats displaying the colors of their master's coat of arms.

"These are my most faithful and hardy knights whom I trust with my life. They help me govern this town in a fair and just manner. I make the laws and they see to it that the laws are enforced. That's why, you see, I can't let your friend go with just a contemptible payment of money. If I did, these fine men would have no respect for me. Instead, your friend must prove to me that he deserves his freedom and since he's locked up, it's up to you to show me."

I gazed at him questioningly and didn't know what to say. What was it that he wanted me to do for him? Was he setting a trap for me? Was he jesting me?

William spoke again. "Let's not talk anymore of your troubled companion until after we eat. Now say hello to my men. This is Sir John, Sir David, Sir Joseph." Each man nodded at me and I nodded at him as his name was spoken. "Sir Arthur, Sir Richard, Sir Stewart, and Sir Walter." Then, clapping his hands, Lord Stanton called to the servants. "Bring out the food!"

While the servants brought out our supper, the priest stood and led everyone in prayer. When he was finished, the holy man gave me a quick chilling glare. I didn't blame him though, for any man of nobility would've felt contempt for a peasant who dined at the high table. I myself greatly wondered why I had been invited to occupy such a high position for the evening. It made me feel awkward and I almost wished I'd been seated at the lowest table.

A moment later, our supper was laid out before us. My mouth watered as I eyed the enormous selection of meats, cheeses, and spicy dipping sauces. There was ham, bacon, duck, pigeon, pheasant, chicken, stew, honey sweetened meats, and cheeses of various colors and textures, much more than we could possibly eat. Of course, whatever was left over from the fine meal wouldn't be wasted; it would be given to the servants. Even our trenchers, the large pieces of stale bread that we used to place our food upon, would be given to the beggars who came by every noble estate after supper.

I reached out and grabbed a fat steaming chicken leg and bit into the succulent flesh. Hot oil squirted from the meat and ran down my chin as its glorious flavor spread throughout my mouth. It had been a long time since I'd tasted fresh meat other than fish and it was wonderful. A few seconds later, I was finished with the leg and I threw the bone to the straw covered floor.

"Ah, so you like it?" asked Lord Stanton as he gnawed on a slab of roast duck.

I nodded my head and grabbed a whole pigeon. For the next few minutes the room was silent except for the sounds of slurping, belching, and tearing meat. I ate a bit of everything that was spread out before me on the huge table and it reminded me of my parents' home and of the grand meals consumed there.

I glanced around while gnawing on a particularly gristly piece of ham and observed that everyone's hands were at their mouths stuffing food into them. I noticed a sizeable chunk of meat in Sir Joseph's beard, which I don't think he was aware of, and more stew on the face of Sir Richard than was in his bowl. Delighted at the sights, I smiled.

Ale was poured for everyone including me, but I didn't touch it. I kept glancing at it though, and as I ate, I became more and more thirsty. Should I have just one drink? I wondered.

I gazed around the room and saw that everyone but me was gulping down the dark brew between each mouthful of food. I wanted so much to take the mug before me and lift it to my lips, but the thought of my drinking and Emery's death wouldn't leave my mind. Suddenly, without thinking, I pushed the mug away.

William and all his knights glanced up from their meal and gaped at me with dumfounded expressions. Sir Walter's beady little eyes glared at me as a shred of pheasant hung from his mouth and the room became deathly still. The only sound came from a piece of meat falling onto the table. It was the chunk of meat that had been stuck in Sir Joseph's beard.

"What's wrong with the ale?" asked Sir John in a voice that quacked like a duck. "Not good enough for you eh?"

I peered around the room and all eyes were on me. I didn't know what to say except to tell the truth. "I don't drink ale."

"Oh, so you drink only wine?" questioned Sir David, whose cheeks resembled a chipmunk's and whose head appeared too small for his body. "How can a poor man afford only wine?"

"No," I objected. "I don't think you understand. I'm a drinkwater!"

"Hmm, strange for a man of your youth," said Lord Stanton, "but you're my guest and what you want or don't want is your decision. Ralph!" he called to a servant. "Fetch this man some water from the well!"

"Yes my lord," replied the servant before exiting the hall.

Everyone resumed eating and I was glad that the uncomfortable situation was over with. No one questioned me further on my reason for not drinking and I was thankful. The servant brought me a pail of water and a fresh mug. I quickly drank down a full glass and filled another.

As I continued to eat, I began to ponder why William, as he had told me to call him, had no wife or family. Had he ever had a wife? I didn't know, and though I was curious, I certainly wasn't going to ask him outright.

Soon, everyone was done with the main meal and we all sat about the table licking our fingers and wiping our faces clean with our tunics. Then to my surprise the servants brought out dates and oranges, an after supper treat affordable only to the extremely wealthy.

After biting into a splendid juicy orange, I threw the peel to the rush-covered floor and noticed it was blanketed with chunks of sinew and bone. It's about time the servants replace the old straw for new, I thought. When I looked up, a fracas was beginning at the end of the table where Sir Arthur and Sir Richard were seated.

"You know it's rude to spit across the table!" shouted the fair-haired Sir Richard.

"I know that!" replied Sir Arthur. "I didn't spit over the table, I spat to the side!"

Lord Stanton stood up. "Alright, that's enough!" he roared, gesturing to his seven knights. "You men clear out of here. You've got work to do before the day's over." The knights glared at each other, downed their mugs of ale, and clambered out of the hall.

For the next hour, William said nothing about what I could do to help free Donovan. Instead, the guests, the priest, Lord Stanton, and I all listened to the two wandering musicians and storytellers whom I had been seated with earlier in the evening. Though I wasn't in the mood for entertainment, they were actually quite good and made me laugh several times.

After the merriment, the guests and the priest thanked Lord Stanton for the great evening and said their good-byes. Soon they were gone and only William and I were left together in the great hall.

William began pacing back and forth in front of the hearth in the middle of the room. The only sound was of that made by the blazing fire. It popped, cracked, and hissed, resembling some strange beast, while its eerie light danced upon the walls.

"Winston, how is it that you've come to speak like the gentry?" asked Lord Stanton unexpectedly.

Though I should have anticipated such a question, it still caught me off guard. I didn't want to tell him the truth for fear that he wouldn't believe me and thus have me turned over to Cyrus Everett. Since my mind was not clouded with ale, I quickly came up with a plausible story. "My father had no noble blood," I said. "He was but a farmer, though a lucky one I should say. Our small cottage was close to our master's manor and he was a good Lord. He had a son the same age as I and we often played together. We became good friends and I grew up around his family, learning all I could from them. They took to me and when I was seven I became a house servant. This gave me an even greater chance to learn. I listened and gained all the knowledge I could from them about anything and everything. That's probably why I speak with some resemblance of a nobleman."

He stopped pacing and stood in front of me. He studied my face for a moment and I tried to appear as believable as possible. It must have worked, for he dropped the subject and went on to another topic.

"Have you ever been in a tournament?"

"No, never." I replied.

"Have you ever used a quintain?"

"Yes, when I was younger, but it was only for fun. The knights at my lord's manor sometimes let me play when they were done practicing." Though my story was a lie, it was true that I had used a quintain before.

"Well then, that settles it," said William as he nestled himself in a chair next to the dancing fire.

I was waiting for him to continue, but he said nothing more. "That settles what?" I asked.

The nobleman quickly gazed up at me, almost as if he were startled. "Oh, sorry, I'm rather tired. What was the question?" I repeated it to him. "Oh yes. I've decided what you must do to get your friend out of confinement."

"And what is that?"

"Once a year we have a tournament here in Hertford. Over the years I've gone up against most everyone here and in the nearby towns and villages. That is, most everyone who's not bedridden or crippled." He laughed heartily and grinned.

I knew what he was about to say, but instead of interrupting I let him continue.

"I propose that you battle me in a tournament, the tilt to be exact. If you win, then you and your friend go free. If you lose, then we shall see."

"But that's unfair!" I protested. "I have no more experience with a lance than does a child!" Actually, I'd had quite a bit of practice with a lance as a squire, but I had no intention of letting him know that.

"You're young and you can learn fast and there's still two weeks until the event. My men will teach you every day until then."

My mind was racing and I didn't know what to say. I must have appeared frightened or troubled, for Lord Stanton spoke again.

"Don't worry lad, this won't be a duel to the death, this is for sport. We'll use a lance of courtesy."

After hearing that, I was much relieved. A lance of courtesy meant that the pointed end would be covered with a rocket, a rounded piece of wood. The object of the sport was only to knock the other off of his horse, not to run him through.

"Well, what do you say? Do you agree?"

"I've not much choice in the matter, do I?"

William smiled. "I'm not holding you here," he answered. "You've done me no wrong. You're free to go at any time, but if you want to free your friend, then this is what you must do."

For a moment I considered leaving Donovan and going on my way, but I had nothing to lose by waiting two more weeks. If anything, I speculated, I might gain some more experience with a lance. "I'll sport you."

"Good, then it's agreed." He stood and reached his hand out and I shook it firmly. "You know," he said, "you remind me of my son. A good strong lad."

I watched him after he spoke. His eyes wandered and a solemn expression overtook him. I wanted to ask him where his son was, but then I realized from the appearance on his face that his son was no longer living.

He cleared his throat and spoke again. "You can eat and sleep here if you'd like. You're my guest and tomorrow, if you want too, you can visit your friend."

"Alright," I agreed.

"Gwendalyn!" William called to a servant who had just passed through the hall that led into the pantry. "Fix this lad a bed by the fire."

"Yes sir," she replied and she hurried off down the hall to gather bedding.

Lord Stanton stood up and rubbed his eyes. "You better get some rest, you've a long day tomorrow with the quintain." He began strolling toward his chamber. "Good night Winston."

"Good night Lord Stanton."

"William," he corrected.

"Good night, William." I said.

Gwendalyn returned with two blankets and a pillow. "Here you go lad, lucky lad I might say."

I scrutinized her leathery old face and she smiled brightly for such a poor old soul. "Why do you say that?" I asked.

"He's taken a liking to you, he has. Now you better get some sleep."

I laid on one of the blankets and she placed the other over me. Habitually, as though she'd done it a million times, she tucked the edges of the blanket in around my body and fluffed the pillow up before laying it under my head. The old lady had a gentle touch and she reminded me of my grandmother who had long since passed away.

"Gwendalyn?" I asked.

"Yes? What is it, my boy?"

"What happened to William's son?"

"Tragic," she said, shaking her head. "Alive one day, gone the next—some sort of illness—took his wife too. Took a few others in town also, but I thank the Lord it wasn't an epidemic."

Then Gwendalyn patted my head in a motherly manner and turned around. Picking up a log, she tossed it on the dying fire. "Goodnight."

CHAPTER SEVEN

The following day I was awoken just after sunrise by Sir David and Sir John. A servant brought us some bread and ale for breakfast. I refused the ale and asked for water. The two knights glared at me strangely and Sir John pushed a mug of brew in front of me. "Drink," he quacked, "it's good for you."

"For you maybe, but for me it's not." I replied, feeling bound and determined to never drink ale again.

The two men frowned at me, glanced at each other, and then shrugged their shoulders.

After breakfast we went outside to the bailey. The bailey was just beyond the inner walls of the castle and contained a stable, an armory, storehouses, a blacksmith's shop, and the barracks for the knights. Surrounding this was the outer walls of the castle.

Near the center of the bailey was a quintain that the knights used to practice their tilting skills. We went over to it and Sir David began explaining its proper use. I was already familiar with the quintain from my days as a squire. It was a tall T-shaped piece of wood where the top of the T swiveled on a pivot so that it could swing freely around. The T-bar was the height of a man on horseback. On one end of it hung a wooden figure wearing a rusty suit of armor while at the other end hung an immense sack of dirt acting as a counterweight.

To practice tilting, a rider would mount his horse in full armor and begin charging the quintain from twenty to thirty yards away. If his horse didn't flinch and if the rider was able to hit the target square on, the counterweight would swing safely behind him. If the rider didn't hit the target directly, the sack of dirt would often knock the man off of his beast. I had felt the pain of that occurrence many times as a squire.

Sir John mounted his destrier and Sir David handed him a lance. The rod was smooth and polished, a little over ten feet long, and made of hard wood. Sir John held the lance close to his right side with the end of it crossing over in front of him and pointing outward to the left of his beast's head. "This is how you hold it when charging. Remember to brace yourself just before impact or you may lose your balance and be knocked off of your horse." He raised the rod perpendicular to the ground and trotted away from us.

When Sir John was about thirty yards from the quintain he motioned to us to step back and we did. He lowered the lance and kicked his spurs into his steed's flanks. The horse galloped toward the quintain and Sir John held steady like a statue. Just before impact he raised his shield with his left arm and pressed his feet back into the stirrups.

A loud bang erupted from the rusty old target as Sir John's lance hit precisely in the center of it. The T-bar swung around and the counterweight just missed him. He quickly turned his horse around, rode toward us, and quacked, "You see it's really quite easy."

"He loves to show off," whispered Sir David to me.

"I heard that!" exclaimed Sir John and we all laughed.

Next, we went to the armory to put together a suit of armor for me. Since armor is usually tailor made for the original owner, it took a long while to find enough old and discarded plates to fit me properly. The blacksmith had to make numerous adjustments, but eventually I was fully fitted.

I quickly found the armor to be heavy and awkward. Twice I clumsily stumbled and fell while on my way back to the quintain. Ignoring the laughter that accompanied each fall, I stood up defiantly and continued onward.

For the rest of that day I practiced tilting with the quintain. I stopped counting how often I was knocked from my horse after the fifteenth time and by the end of the day I felt as though I'd been beaten by twenty men. I had bruises and cuts over my entire body and I eagerly awaited that evening's rest.

I didn't see Lord Stanton the whole day nor at supper. During supper the house servants told me that their master had gone to visit a Baron in another town. The whereabouts of my host didn't concern me at all, for I was too hungry and tired to care. I ate ravenously and retired early next to the warm fire in the great hall.

It was well after dawn the following morning when a sunbeam reached in through a window to open my eyes. My body was stiff and sore from the prior day's activity and I could barely stretch my muscles without wincing in pain. I didn't want to practice with the lance and quintain, but I knew I would have too. Then I remembered that Lord Stanton had told me I could visit Donovan if I wanted too. In all the excitement of the day before, I had forgotten.

At breakfast I asked Sir David, who was nibbling at his food like a rodent, if I could visit Donovan. He agreed that I could, but I would have to practice with him and Sir John again in the afternoon. When we were through eating, the two knights accompanied me to the dungeon.

The steps to the dungeon were made from huge stone blocks and the air became cool and dank as I descended them. Water dripped from the walls and ceiling, and there was barely enough light to see.

The door to Donovan's cell was rusty and screeched noisily as Sir David opened it. The cell itself was much brighter than I'd anticipated due to a broad barred window that ran just above ground level along the top of the dungeon's outer wall.

"My lad! Good to see you!" These were the first words that came from Donovan's fleshy lips. He stood up and gave me a hug and then shook my hand. "I see they've gotten a hold of you too—the dirty rogues!" Then he glared at the two knights and snarled, "I've done nothing and neither has the lad! It's nothing but lies I tell you! I'm a personal friend to the king and he shall hear about this!"

"Donovan, calm down!" I exclaimed. "These men aren't bringing me here to be locked up! I was brought here at my own request so I could speak to you!"

"We'll be back in awhile," Sir John broke in, "just call for us if you need anything."

"Of course," I replied as they clamored off down the hall.

"You mean they really haven't arrested you? You're here of your own free will?" Donovan asked with an air of surprise.

"Yes, I know you wouldn't do it for me, but I'm staying here to help free you."

Donovan gaped at me in amazement. "I thought you'd be in London by now. Why would you stay here in a strange village to help a man you don't even know?"

"I can't tell you," I said, "because I don't know myself. I thought about continuing on to London, but something drew me here. How have you been treated?"

"Good—almost too good. It makes me nervous when a lord feeds his prisoners so well. I feel like a pig being fattened for slaughter."

"Well, from what I've seen, he's fair and just, and treats all men with respect."

"It sounds like you're defending him. He may feed me well, but he's still got me locked up in this damn dungeon!"

A wave of anger flushed through Donovan's pudgy face and I tried to calm him. "Settle down! Remember I'm here to get you out." I gestured toward his bedding of straw. "May I sit?"

He nodded.

We both nestled ourselves down into the pile of straw and I told Donovan how at first I had offered Lord Stanton money and he refused it. Then I told him of the upcoming tournament and how if I won we could go free.

"And what if you lose?"

"I don't plan on losing," I replied.

"But if you do, that's when we'll pay the piper. That's when we find out what evil lurks in the man's heart whom you've befriended."

"No, he's not like that!" I exclaimed. "For some reason he likes me. I believe I remind him of his son who is with him no more."

"Let's pray you're right," Donovan muttered as he made the sign of the cross over his chest.

*   *   *

Lord Stanton returned from his business travel the following day and for the next week and a half I practiced with the quintain while Donovan was kept in the dungeon. With each passing day I felt myself becoming stronger and more confident. The knights of the castle were amazed at how quickly I learned. My blows were fast and accurate and all agreed that I must have had royal blood in my lineage somewhere. A couple of the knights even went so far as to say that I might actually beat Lord Stanton in the tilt. Of course none of them knew how much experience I'd had before as a squire, so there was reason for them to believe I was a quick learner. They hadn't a clue of how close I'd actually become to being knighted.

How close indeed I recalled one hot afternoon while practicing with Sir John. So close I could almost taste it, but that was before the ale had completely taken over my thoughts and deeds—before my master sent me home in disgrace to my father—before the word drunkard became synonymous in the town of Dereham with the name Winston Tabor.

As my mind reeled with these convictions a bitter taste rose in my mouth and I swallowed hard. I charged the quintain with all the speed I could muster from my steed and hit the target with such force that it broke off from the T-bar. This relieved some of the pent up anger and disgust I had for myself at that moment and left me in a better disposition. Practice for the day was curtailed by this event and Sir John gave me the rest of the afternoon off.

Later that day, only five days before the tournament, William received an unexpected message. He told me that he and all his knights must go to a neighboring town to help catch a small band of criminals who had escaped from Baron Gadberry's dungeon. He explained that he really didn't want to go because Baron Gadberry was a cruel master and most of the men who had escaped probably didn't deserve to be incarcerated. Lord Stanton was obliged to go though, because his own master, the Duke of Hertfordshire, was also the overseer of Baron Gadberry. Since William was the Duke's vassal and had given him an oath of loyalty, he had to respond when called upon by the Duke.

Before leaving, Lord Stanton told me that I could do whatever I wanted while he was away. He handed me the key to Donovan's cell and said, "If you wish to talk to your friend, by all means, go ahead. You have the run of the castle. I will be back in time for the tilt." Then he turned and strode out of the great hall in which I stood.

I was astounded. How could he trust me with the key to Donovan's cell while he and his knight's were away? How did he know I wouldn't steal whatever I could and leave with Donovan?

For the rest of that day I wandered about town visiting shops and greeting townsfolk who were busy with their daily toil. All the while I kept an eye out for anyone following me. I figured that William and his men must have been setting a trap for me. I wanted to know why this strange man would leave me alone in his castle with a key to his dungeon and only his house servants to watch me.

In the evening I went back to the manor and the servants fed me supper. After the meal, I rested by the cozy fire in the great hall till late into the night. During that time, my thoughts were muddled and I wondered whether I should go to the dungeon and free Donovan and be on my way.

That's probably what Lord Stanton wanted me to do, I postulated. Then he could arrest me and do what it was he wanted to do with me. He was up to something I was sure, but exactly what it was I did not know.

Before falling asleep that night, I resolved my inner conflict enough to come to a decision. I would stay as a guest of William's until the tournament was over. After all, I had been treated fairly if not admirably by him during the entire length of my unplanned visit. Just because he was unusual and overly agreeable did not make him a criminal. He really gave me no reason to believe that he had an ulterior motive to keep me at his castle.

The following day I didn't dare visit Donovan for I knew he would try to talk me into leaving. I was already too indecisive about what I should do and speaking with him would have misguided my own judgment.

I resolved to focus my thoughts on other matters for a while, so I fitted myself in the armor I'd been lent and headed out to the stable. With help from the stable-master, I mounted my horse and began practicing with the lance and quintain.

My mind was clear and my reflexes were quick as I rode back and forth pounding the quintain with my rod. I was hitting the target with every blow now and after a week and a half of practice, I felt I was ready to tilt with the best of them. I knew my youth and agility would help offset Lord Stanton's skill and experience.

When I was done, I wandered back into the castle. Gwendalyn, the old maid, had a pot of cabbage soup bubbling over the waning fire and some bread on the table for her and the other servants.

"Winston, you may have a cooked chicken or anything else," she said with a smile that brought attractiveness to her aged wrinkled face. "My lord said you could have whatever you want. That he did."

Smelling the cabbage soup brought warmth to my soul and it reminded me of Emery and his humble cozy cabin. I pictured the stream that flowed by the old man's shack and I could see Emery working in his garden. Then I saw Meranda. Oh Meranda, if only I could hold you in my arms and gaze into your—

"Winston, do you hear me?"

I gazed up from my daydream to see the gentle face of the old maid. "Soup and bread is fine," I replied as my mind concentrated upon more immediate needs, mainly hunger.

Gwendalyn placed a bowl of soup in front of me and I slurped it up with hardly a breath between gulps. The second bowl I sipped a bit slower while dipping a sizeable piece of bread into it and biting off each juicy chunk with delight.

After supper, with my hunger satiated, I became restless. There was no one to play games with since all the servants were busy making preparations for the upcoming tournament. I thumbed through a few manuscripts that William kept in the great hall, but they held my interest for only a minute or two. I considered visiting Donovan in his cell, but I decided against it fearing again that he might talk me into something I would regret later. Eventually, I found myself wandering upstairs in the solar near the master's quarters.

As I passed William's chamber, a great urge to enter came over me. I glanced around and saw no one, so I quickly stepped in through the open doorway.

In a corner of the room rested two open trunks filled with clothes and in another sat a bench and a small table. In between them, hung upon the wall, was an enormous coverlet with a picture of the Virgin Mary holding the baby Jesus. Underneath this was a finely carved wooden bed covered with thick lavish blankets. Next to the bed was a distinctive chest with rich embroidery along its sides. I tiptoed over to examine it closer.

The chest was similar to the one my father had kept his coins and jewelry within. I grabbed a handle on one end and tried to lift it. It was remarkably heavy for its size and I was barely able to raise it an inch off of the floor. It would have taken at least four strong men to move it to another room. I presumed it was locked, but upon closer inquiry I noticed that the lid was ajar.

I gazed quickly toward the entrance of the room to make sure no one was watching me. Then I stood silent for a moment and listened for any noise my ears might detect. There was none.

My brow grew wet with sweat and a shiver shot up my spine. I knew what I was doing was wrong and if I were caught I'd surely join Donovan in the dungeon, but at that moment I didn't care. My spirit was full of excitement like a child who is given a present and just has to open it then and there to know what's inside.

I pulled on the lid and it opened easily. What I had suspected was true; it was Lord Stanton's fortune, more silver and gold than I'd ever seen. There was at least twenty times the amount of coins that had ever passed through my father's hands.

In the middle of all the coins was a wooden box. I reached down to open it and inside were necklaces, rings, earrings, and bracelets, all elaborately detailed. They must have been made by the finest of craftsmen, yet they were badly tarnished as though they hadn't been taken care of for some time.

Could these be the jewels of his widow? I wondered. Why would he keep them after her death and not sell them? Why would such a rich and youthful looking Lord as himself not remarry? Could he have cherished his wife so much as to love no other women ever again?

I thought of Meranda and pictured her radiant face and sparkling blue eyes. Yes, I understood how a man could love a woman so. I would treasure Meranda in the same manner if I were ever given the chance. An immense feeling of joy came over me as I recalled the pleasant times spent with the lovely peasant girl I had come to know.

With a smile on my lips, I rested on the edge of Lord Stanton's bed and placed the tarnished jewelry back into the wooden box and set it atop the pile of coins inside the chest. I was about to close the lid on the fortune in front of me and leave the room when an evil idea interrupted my cheery mood.

My eyes focused sharply on the pile of coins before me and I turned toward the entrance of the room. No one was there. Then, reaching my hands into the treasure, I picked up a pile of cold hard coins and let them trickle through my fingers.

If I took but a tenth of these coins I'd be rich, I reasoned. I could leave from here tonight and be on my way to London. Lord Stanton and his men wouldn't be back at least until tomorrow and I'd be far away by then. I could—

The schemes came cascading so quickly that my mind was clouded with greed. I began heaping coins into my tunic and for that moment all I cared about was how much gold and silver I could carry away. Handful after handful I stuffed into my tunic until my pockets bulged and overflowed with coins.

Suddenly, halfway through my fiendish act, I stopped and stood silent for a moment. What was that? I strained my ears and gazed toward the door. Sweat trickled down my forehead and my body swayed back and forth with each beat of my heart. Footsteps echoed from down the hall and they became louder with every step.

I couldn't move, for if I did, the coins in my pocket would jingle and surely give me away. My legs twitched with restlessness and a drop of sweat fell from the tip of my nose. I stood silent and dormant like a volcano ready to explode.

Why did I let myself get in this predicament? Why was I so greedy? If only I had never entered this room. If only—

The footsteps seemed so loud that each one rang in my head like a church bell. I knew I was only seconds away from being discovered by one of the servants. Suddenly, the shadow of a figure flashed through the doorway and fell across the floor. This is it—to the dungeon they'll take me! But the shadow was only a passing one, and the footsteps began to fade as briskly as they had come.

I wiped the sweat from my forehead and began replacing the coins, which I had so greedily taken, back into the chest. When I was done, I closed the lid and quickly left the room.

CHAPTER EIGHT

It was early in the morning on the day before the tournament when Lord Stanton and his men returned. They had succeeded in capturing most of the prisoners who had escaped from Baron Gadberry's dungeon. The remaining fugitives, I was told, would likely be apprehended soon, for they were only on foot and Gadberry's hounds were hot on their trail.

"Are you ready for the tilt tomorrow?" Lord Stanton asked me as he sauntered into the great hall where I was eating breakfast.

"The question is—are you?" I asked.

He chuckled and winked at me saying, "We shall see. We shall see." Then, turning toward his knights, he spoke again. "But first we must prepare for the guests who shall arrive today. I'm already behind on my time, so leave me now and attend to your chores." The men left the great hall and Lord Stanton headed upstairs to his solar.

After breakfast, I moved closer to the large hearth and nestled down beside the crackling fire. As I warmed myself, I watched the house servants who were busy cooking, cleaning, and preparing rooms for the guests to stay in. The noblest visitors would be fortunate enough to reside in the castle during the tournament. Those of gentler birth would stay in tents in the meadow near the tilting grounds or wherever they could find room.

Just before noon Lord Stanton came to me and said, "Lad, in order to be correct with the rules of the tournament, you must be a knight or at least an armiger to participate. So, I grant you status as an armiger. My men tell me you deserve at least that by the way you handle a lance."

"Thank you sir," I replied, wanting to tell him that I already was an armiger, but knowing that I couldn't.

"I've not had time to select a sword to present to you as I should, but when I have a chance I will get one for you."

"Thank you again sir, but I've no need of a sword, I've got one here which I've become accustomed to." I motioned to the blade on my hip.

"Yes, I've noticed you've kept that leather hilt sword quite close to you at all times. I've a feeling you know how to use it too." He smiled.

"Come, the guests will be arriving soon and we must be ready to greet them."

We left the great hall's smoke and darkness behind and strolled outside into the courtyard. Again the courtyard amazed me with its striking beauty as it had the first time I saw it. The cobblestone walk, the gardens, and the statues of the saint's created such a placid scene that if a person were alone he might possibly forget the daily burdens of everyday life.

William gestured for me to take a seat and we both rested ourselves on a marble bench, the same one I had seen the young girls sitting on when I had first come to the castle. While thinking of those fair maidens, I blurted out, "Have you any daughters?" and the moment the last word left my tongue I realized the question was absurd. I had never heard nor had I seen any evidence that William had any daughters. The thought had simply entered my mind and my mouth had taken action before I could put a stop to it.

Lord Stanton gazed at me thoughtfully. "No, no I don't. I wish I had, but my wife bore me but one child, a son, before she passed away."

After telling me this, I saw an awful pain in William's face as though I had opened an old wound. Instantly I wished I hadn't broached the subject at all.

William must have sensed my discomfort. "It's okay lad," he said, slapping a hand on my knee. "I loved my wife and my son as much as any man ever could. When they died, I nearly died too. I almost gave up on life completely, but I pulled through it. Somehow, God let me know that my wife and son were okay. I only hope that when it's time for me to leave this world, I might join them in heaven."

As he spoke, I gazed at Lord Stanton and he appeared much older than his usual youthful self. His eyes were red and watery, and as he wiped them with the sleeves of his surcoat, I noticed that there were strands of gray in his mostly raven black curly hair.

William suddenly stood and cleared his throat. "So, you were hoping I had daughters? Isn't that just the sort of thing a young man would want to know."

"When I first came here," I replied, glad that William had moved the topic away from his deceased wife and son, "there were three ladies here in the court yard. If you don't mind me asking, who were they?"

"Ah, I believe they were the three daughters of the Duke of Winterburry. He had come on business and they had accompanied him. I know what you're thinking, but I'm sorry, they won't be here for the tournament."

"That's alright," I said quickly, feeling a bit embarrassed, "it's just that they had reminded me of someone, that's all."

"A girl, yes? So you've been smitten by love already. Where is this young lady?"

"Far away," I answered, "and I shall probably not see her ever again for she was not partial to me—for good cause I believe. Anyway, it's a long story and I'm not in the mood to tell it."

"Why you sound like an old man!" exclaimed Lord Stanton. "You're but what—twenty years at most—and you've given up? The world is small and you shall see her again."

"I hope you're right," I said with a sigh, "but to me she seems far enough away to be in another world."

"Yes, and what a world you've come from," replied Lord Stanton with a strange twinkle in his dark eyes.

His comment was disconcerting and caught me off guard, but my concerns were quickly diverted when suddenly the trumpeters began blowing their horns signaling the arrival of the guests.

The gates to the courtyard were thrown open and an ensemble of knights and their ladies entered. The knights rode festively upon their prancing steeds, their armor gleaming in the late morning sun, as their ladies strode along beside them. Joining them also were their pages, squires, and servants carrying supplies and equipment.

When the fanfare was over and the knights had dismounted, Lord Stanton greeted each man, woman, and child with his charming manner and offered them drink for their dry pallets. Then, depending on their noble stature, the guests were led by the servants to their quarters or were shown where they could set up camp. Though I don't know why, Lord Stanton asked me to stay with him as he greeted the guests, introducing me by my first name only and as an armiger from a noble family from Wales. This I pondered, but I did not question.

While receiving the visitors, I noticed that the gentry who came for the tournament were not as high ranking as many of those who had attended the few contests I had seen with my family, but the affair was not meant to be a large one. Most tournaments celebrated a holiday, the knighting of a son of a great nobleman, or some other important event. This competition was celebrated for none of those reasons that I was aware of. It appeared only to be a yearly match that the lord put on mainly for his and his townsfolk's delight. Another difference between this contest and most, was that many tournaments lasted for two or three days and the guests were invited months in advance from all over the country. This engagement was to last for only a day and the gentry who came were from local towns and villages. They knew each other, some very well, and they probably did business with each other on a daily basis. It was more like a gathering of close friends than a huge spectacle of pomp and bravura, but still it was exciting.

Once all the guests had arrived, set up their tents, and settled in, it was just after dark. There was no special supper served and everyone retired early, for all would be up before dawn. I slept on some rushes by the hearth in the main hall covered by a warm wool blanket. Being exhausted from meeting all the people earlier in the day, I slumbered easily.

I awoke before daybreak to the clamor of the servants as they set up the tables for the morning meal. When breakfast was ready, the guests who had stayed in the castle came to the hall and were served bread and bacon. The visitors who had camped outside in the nearby meadow would have to supply their own food and drink for breakfast, though in the evening everyone would be invited to the feast provided by Lord Stanton.

It was a cheery gathering round the tables that morning. Mouths were busy talking as bread and bacon were being stuffed into them. Ale, mead, and tea flowed freely from the pitchers of the attending servants.

I took a seat by a gentleman I didn't recognize. He was thin but not fragile in appearance and he wore a mustache and goatee, which gave him a fiendish air. While studying his face for a moment, his eyes caught mine and he spoke.

"Good morning to you son. Don't believe we've met. My name's Gadberry, Baron Gadberry." He curled his lips into a devilish grin and stuck out his long slender hand to shake.

"Winston Tabor," I said, placing my hand in his. I shook his limp cold hand firmly and then wiped off the sweat he'd left on my fingers onto my surcoat.

"Sir Tabor, should I call you?" he asked.

"No, I've not been knighted yet, though I am an armiger."

"Then you'll be in the mock battle today?"

"No," I answered him, "I believe I will tilt against only one man, Lord Stanton."

"Ah ha ha ha ha ha ha! So, William has run out of local men to tilt with eh? You know he's beaten every man within a hundred miles. Hope you knock him on his backside!"

"I'll sure try," I said.

"Sure you will son," he replied, before curling his lips into a hideous smile.

There was something detestable about the man. I wished I hadn't sat by him, but since I had and not wanting to be discourteous, I continued with the small talk. "I don't remember seeing you yesterday. May I ask when you arrived?"

"Late last night, most everyone was asleep."

"Yes, that's right," I said, remembering that it was Baron Gadberry whom William and his men had gone to help catch the fugitives. "You were after those men. Did you catch the last of them?"

He gazed at me with a blank stare as if I'd spoken an unknown language. "What's that you say? I don't believe I heard you right," he said.

The room had become noisy with so many people chatting, so I spoke louder. "The men you were after—the ones that Lord Stanton came to help you catch—did you get them all?"

"I've not a clue of what you're talking about son. I haven't seen William for at least two months."

As his words trailed off, my mouth fell open in disbelief. It was obvious that the man, no matter how deceiving he appeared, was telling the truth. He really hadn't seen Lord Stanton recently.

"What's wrong son? You okay?"

I looked up and the man's appearance startled me. I nearly expected to see horns growing from his temples and fangs sticking out between his lips. "Yes, I'm fine," I replied. "I must have mixed you up with someone else, that's all."

"Yes, you must have," he said, before turning his head and gazing at me strangely from the corner of one eye. Then he twisted his chair away from me and began talking to the man on his left.

Quickly, I glanced around the tables to find Lord Stanton. He was across the room and when our eyes met I must have given him a disquieting glare, for he suddenly appeared disturbed. His left brow lifted up in a questioning manner as if to ask, "What have I done to deserve that look?" After breakfast he would find out, I thought.

When the meal was over, I shook Baron Gadberry's cold sweaty hand again and told him I was happy to have met him. This was a lie of course, but it would have been callow to tell him he looked like the devil in human form.

When breakfast was over, most of the guests began drifting away from the tables and headed in the direction of the estate's chapel for mass. I met Lord Stanton, who was busy chatting with a few of the visitors, at the entrance to the chapel. I suppose I shouldn't have bothered him at such a time, but he had lied to me about where he had been during the previous days and I wanted to know why.

"Sir, can I see you for a moment?" I asked.

"Yes," he replied before excusing himself from his guests. "Come with me," he said.

I followed him and he led me back to the great hall, up through the solar, and into his chamber.

"Sit," he directed as he perched himself down on the edge of his bed and motioned me toward a bench. "I think I know what you want, but I shall let you ask me to be sure."

"You were not at Baron Gadberry's the last few days. You haven't even seen him for two months. Am I correct?"

"Yes."

"Then why did you lie?" I questioned him angrily. "I've caused you no trouble! I only came here to help a friend—not even a friend—just a man I met on the road. Why did I do it? I don't know! Maybe because I hoped someone would do the same for me if I were in trouble. How do I know you'll ever let Donovan go? I don't really! It seems to me you've kept me here for nothing more than amusement, but worst of all, I began to trust you! Now I've lost that and I don't know what to think of you anymore!"

When I was finished the room fell silent. William sat placidly on his bed as if he had been prepared for every word I had spoken during my outburst. Many a Lord would have thrown me in the dungeon for the way I had voiced myself toward him.

"I'm sorry," he said. "You're right, I have meant to keep you here longer than you've wanted to stay, but not for amusement. I must confess, you remind me of my son and I've missed his companionship, but you are not my son. You cannot take the place of my son and I must accept that. I admire your humanity to help a man whom you hardly know. A man who, if he were in your shoes, would have been gone long ago."

I listened to William and knew what he was saying was not a fabrication. He was speaking from his heart and from it came grief for the son he no longer had. With each word his lips moved in a tedious manner and his face now appeared ashen gray.

"I've missed my son for many years. He would have been about your age now. He was so pure and simple—as you seem to be. I guess I wanted to believe that you were my son, but a week ago a visitor came to call." He paused for a moment and his weary eyes met mine.

"Yes," I said, "go on."

William took in a deep breath and continued. "A man came asking many questions. He wanted to know if I'd seen a young man, a stranger. He described a lad with an appearance similar to you. He told me that the youth was wanted for murdering his father, Lord of Dereham, and that a reward was offered."

"What did you tell him?"

"Don't worry Winston, I didn't mention your name and I told my men to keep quiet about you until I could obtain more information. I'm sorry I lied to you but I had to find out the truth for myself. My men and I traveled to Dereham and made a number of inquiries there. We concluded that the most recent Lord of Dereham, Cyrus Everett, is a ruthless man. He is likely the cause of your father's death and a probable cause in the fatal accident of your mother. He keeps—"

"What? What did you say?" I glared at Lord Stanton intensely and though I had actually heard clearly what he had said, I couldn't believe it. I needed to hear it again.

William must have perceived this, for he took a deep breath and said, "I'm sorry. You didn't know about your mother, did you?"

The truth suddenly hit me and I felt like I'd been punched in the gut by a giant. I sank in my seat. "How did it happen?" I muttered.

"The stairs, supposedly she fell down the stairs and hit her head. Cyrus was the only witness. The town's folk are very suspicious of him now, but no one will confront him. They're afraid of him and his band of cutthroats who rule the village. I'm sorry—"

"No, don't feel pity for me!" I exclaimed. "Have pity on the man who has done this to my family, for I will smile broadly when I cut him open and send his soul to hell!" I trembled with rage for a moment and then slowly I tried to regain my composure. "Go on, tell me more," I stammered.

William furrowed his brow as if wondering whether I was in complete control of myself or not. "Well," he continued, "from the information the visitor had given me, I had no idea whether you truly had or had not killed your father. So, when I left to investigate, I also left my two knights, David and John, to watch over you though you weren't aware of their presence. I suspected that if you truly were a criminal, you would try to steal something and then leave, but you did no such thing."

I immediately recalled the evening just two days before when I had been in the same room I was in now and I had almost stolen William's treasure. I was fortunate that I had had a second chance that night to rethink my greedy intentions. Sir David and Sir John must certainly have been near the castle if not somewhere inside.

Lord Stanton proceeded. "You were here when I returned and on your own free will I might add. It was a test I guess you might say. It was wrong and I realize that now. I believe you're innocent and as an apology to you, you may go freely on your way, with your friend too. You need not tilt with me and I will supply you a fresh horse to take along with you wherever you may go."

Expressionless, I gazed at him. I was upset with the way I had been treated, but he seemed sincerely regretful for his actions and he was trying to make amends. I wasn't exactly sure what to say to him.

"I know what you must do and I know it is your own battle that you must fight," he said, "but if ever you're in need of anything, just let me know. I'll be there for you my son."

As those words trailed off of his lips, I realized that I had gained a great and important ally. A wave of respect and compassion flowed within me for him. "Come," I said, "we have a match to keep."

He glared at me, puzzled. "What?"

"It's time to tilt!" I exclaimed.

"Truly?"

I nodded.

He smiled and a moment later his face had regained its youthful composure that I was so familiar with. "Well then," he said, "we better get to mass, though I believe it's nearly over by now."

We rushed downstairs and dashed across the courtyard to the chapel entrance opposite the larder. When we arrived, we found that mass was over and the last of the guests were strolling out the doors. Just then Sir Richard came out of the chapel and greeted William and I.

"Sir Richard," said Lord Stanton, "would you go to the dungeon and bring Winston's friend to the tournament with you?"

"Of course, right away sir," replied the knight.

"Good, I'm sure the fellow would like to see his captor get beaten by his young friend here." William motioned to me with his hand.

"That's not a thing to be joking about sir, at least not with this lad," said Sir Richard, his face cracked with a grin. "If you asked Sir David or Sir John to place a wager, I couldn't guarantee they'd put their money on you sir."

William laughed robustly. "Is that so? Well, I'm bound to lose someday. Better to lose to a young strong lad than to another old man like myself." He cackled at his own words.

A moment later, after Lord Stanton's laughter had died down, we entered the chapel and knelt at the altar. I prayed for the souls of my father and mother, for Emery, for William's wife and son, and for the safety of all those attending the tournament that day. I asked God to give me the strength and courage to stay away from ale and for the chance to see Meranda again. Also I asked that he give me the opportunity to right the wrongs caused by Cyrus Everett. "Amen," I whispered when I finished, remaining on my knees till Lord Stanton was done.

When he was finished, William stood and said, "Let's go my lad. Today shall be a day of festivity and tonight we shall feast."

We left the chapel with an air of anticipation, practically running to the stable to mount our horses. As we galloped to the lists, the broad grassy field on the west side of town where the tournament was being held, I couldn't help but feel a great sense of excitement. When we arrived, we dismounted our beasts and gave them to William's squires to attend to. For a moment, I stood and gazed in wonder at the whole display before me. It had been a long time since I'd been to a tournament and now I was actually going to be a participant.

Encompassing the lists was an oblong fence and beyond that were wooden platforms with rows of seats which had been erected for the spectators to view the action from. For the gentry, distinctive canopied pavilions had been built. They were decorated with brightly colored shields and banners, and from them hung flowing pennons.

Near the center of the stands, on one of the longer sides, a special platform had been erected for the ladies. In the middle of the platform was the seat for the Queen of Love and Beauty who would hand out the prizes to the winners when the match was over.

At each end of the lists were knights with their squires and pages preparing for the mock battle. Their tents were pitched nearby, each with a pennant fluttering in the breeze showing their coat-of-arms.

Lord Stanton had had a wooden hutch built and it was ready for our use when we arrived. It was in the middle of the stands across the field from where the Queen of Love and Beauty sat. William and I would not be participating in the mock battle, which was the first event, so we climbed up the platform to our seats.

By this time, most everyone was seated and a trumpet blew signifying the beginning of the contest. The morning sun shone brightly on the heralds as they marched through the lane of tents at each end of the lists yelling, "Present yourselves knights! Come forth and fight!"

A procession began from each side of the field. The challengers were to our left and the challenged on our right. They entered the lists on horseback, two by two, with their squires following behind them on foot. The horses pranced with each step they took while the knights, their armor and shields polished and gleaming, were perched motionless on their mounts like statues. They held their lances high in the air and from them fluttered ribbons and scarves worn in honor of their ladies.

As the procession circled around the field so that everyone could get a good look, cheers and applause came pouring from the pavilions and stands. The ladies, dressed in their colorful gowns, waved to their own special knights as they trotted by. Most of the common folk crowded up against the fence surrounding the lists while others climbed nearby trees or stood on carts to get a view.

Soon, the marshal of the tournament took his place in the center of the field. He was accompanied by the heralds who acted as his assistants to help judge and keep score. The marshal declared all to be silent while the rules were being read.

The rules were nearly the same for most tournaments. First and foremost was the rule that the lance could not be pointed or sharpened, although this order was often neglected in towns where feuding was common. Points were given to each contestant for every lance that he broke while using it against his opponent. A great number of points were given if a knight knocked another off of his destrier, but points would be taken away if a knight hit another below the belt. Squires were allowed only to help recover a fallen knight or bring a fresh lance to their master. They couldn't mount a steed and do battle for their lord if he could no longer fight.

After reading the rules, the trumpets blared and the marshal exclaimed, "Fearless knights, in the presence of God, engage in battle!"

A great thunder of pounding hoofs rang out as the two armies rushed toward each other as fast as they could fly. Excitement and apprehension rushed through my veins. Seconds seemed like minutes as I waited for the impact to occur. All the spectators stood up just as the two companies were about to collide. A great resounding crash rumbled through the lists as lances and shields, men and beasts, intertwined to form a mass of metal, wood, and flesh. Half the men on either side were knocked to the earth and a great cloud of dust filled the air making it difficult to see what was happening.

The crowd leaped in delight yelling and clapping with excitement, many hoping their favorite knight would quickly recover. I saw in front of me a young lady tearing the sleeve from her gown and throwing it out into the field. "For you my love! Do me honor with your bravery!" she cried out.

When the dust cleared, men could be seen climbing back on their mounts or being carried off by their squires. The knights who were still able to ride returned to their end of the field and were given fresh lances along with a moment to rest.

"Good show, don't you think?" asked Lord Stanton.

"Yes, really quite good," I replied, though I did feel a bit of pity for the poor men who were being helped off of the field.

The trumpets sounded again and within seconds the earth shook from the galloping of horses. A number of broken lances were strewn on the field, causing some of the animals to stumble as they charged each other. It was a sight to behold as the cracking of wood and smashing of metal rang out again. The dust rose and settled, leaving more men strewn out upon the ground. Some of them limped away while others were carried off bleeding from their mouths and spitting teeth.

Three more times the trumpets blared and three more times the crash of lance upon shield was heard. Then the mock battle was over and everyone cheered, hoping their favorite knight had won. The winners wouldn't be declared until that evening after all the points had been added up by the marshal and his heralds.

The next event was the tilt in which William and I would be participating. There were several matches before we would compete, so we stayed in the stands until it was time for us to prepare.

The fundamental principle of the tilt was to knock one's opponent completely off of his horse and on to the ground. If after five tries neither were thrown from their beast, the winner would be decided by how many blows each contestant had made and how many lances each had broken.

To the victor went the spoils, and the spoils were the defeated knight's armor and horse. The winner could then ransom these items back to the losing knight for money. In this way, not only could a knight gain skill, which he might later need in a real battle, but also an impoverished knight with exceptional ability could eventually become quite rich.

Of course, if Lord Stanton beat me in the tilt, he wouldn't gain a thing, for I was going to ride one of his horses and use his armor. He was engaging in the tilt for sport only. I had heard from his men and from his servants that he had received first prize many times in the mock battles, but that he hadn't participated in them for some time now. Instead, in recent years, he had only tilted once in each tournament and, so far I was told, he had never lost.

The first two tilts we watched were uneventful and the victor would be decided later in the evening after the judges counted up their scores. When the third tilt was about to start, the two participants rode spectacularly onto the field.

From the right, came a knight on a gray and white horse. His armor sparkled delightfully in the sunlight and his beast appeared to dance over the dry dusty earth. From the left, came a dark brown stallion trotting briskly but not gracefully and atop of him rode a knight whose exceptionally polished armor was black. From his helmet fluttered a bright red ribbon, probably worn in honor of his lady.

"He reminds me of the Dark Knight!" yelled William above the clamor of the crowd.

I gave Lord Stanton a questioning glance. It seemed I had heard that name before, but I couldn't quite place it.

Pointing to the man on the left, Lord Stanton shouted, "Haven't you heard of him?"

Then I remembered. "Yes, a legend of some kind I think. My father used to tell me stories about him. That man does appear to be how I would imagine him."

"Your right," William replied. "He looks similar, but he's not the real man."

The trumpets blared again and the marshal began to introduce the two knights.

"Of course he's not the real man!" I shouted over the roar of the crowd. "He's only a fable!"

"No my lad, he lives! And any man who pays his price can hire him for his service, but he is evil. He cares nothing about chivalry—only about riches. He would kill the most noble of men if paid enough to do so. I've often wondered what it would be like to face him in battle."

Just then the marshal called out for the two knights to begin, and with a thunderclap of hoofs they came crashing down upon each other. A resounding crack and splintering of wood roared out across the lists. The knight on the gray and white horse had scored a point by breaking his lance on his opponent's shield. The man in black had missed his foe, but he was still seated firmly on his mount.

"You really believe in the Dark Knight?" I asked William, not absolutely sure if he was jesting me or if he truly believed in the man.

"Yes," he replied, "and about this I would not lie." Then he took his eyes from me and planted them on the field where the knights were circling back around to their starting positions.

The knight who had broken his lance received a new one from his squire and readied himself for the next charge. The marshal gave the signal and the men were off. Within seconds, the two warriors were but a few yards away from each other. The knight in black armor, his red ribbon flying in the wind, aimed his lance carefully for the breast of his opponent. His opponent appeared to be having difficulty with his lance, for he was peering down at his hands and fumbling with the lengthy pole. Fortunately, he glanced up in time and was able to protect himself with his shield before the black horseman's lance struck him. A blaring snap echoed from the dark warrior's rod as it split apart on the struggling knight's shield.

To everyone's horror, the lance broke lengthwise leaving a jagged point at the end. The sharp tip slid along and then off of the side of the gray and white knight's shield, striking him. It entered between his left breast and shoulder plates of armor and ripped into his shoulder and arm. The crowd screamed in dismay as crimson gushed from the wound and the warrior's arm hung awkwardly to his side. Both men halted their steeds and the injured man cast off his helmet. His face was ghostly white.

The marshal and his heralds rushed up to the knight and helped him off of his horse. With blood still pouring from his injury, they carried him from the field and into the marshal's tent.

The scenario brought back memories of when I was a young lad with my father. In most contests mishaps were to be expected. Cuts, bruises, broken teeth and the like were all part of the sport. Sadly though, no matter how much armor a knight wore, there were often one or two men who were maimed or killed. It still made me feel sick to my stomach as it had when I was child.

"Come my lad, it's time to prepare."

"What?" I asked, turning to Lord Stanton. "Oh yes, I'd forgotten for a moment."

"Don't worry Winston, what we just saw rarely happens. Now let's go have some fun."

Right, I thought, let's go have some fun, as long as neither of us gets killed!

William's servants had our armor ready and our horses equipped for us when we arrived at the tent. Lord Stanton's pages and squires had seen to it that their master would look splendid for the tournament. His metal was polished so well that it was hard to gaze upon him for more than an instant without the reflection from the sun hurting my eyes.

William's servants helped me put on my armor, which was far from spectacular. It too had recently been polished, but blemishes and rusty discolorations were still clearly visible over the entire outfit.

When it was almost time for the tilt, William mounted his horse, as did I. "I'll go around to the other side," he said, trotting away with his squires following behind. "Good luck Winston!"

I nodded and waited for the heralds to motion me out into the field. When they finally did, I entered the lists and saw that William was at the other end. We proceeded to march our horses around the field, as had all of the prior participants, so that the crowd could cheer for their favorite contestant.

As I moved along the platforms where the gentry were seated, I peered up at them. Not one of them was waving or cheering for me. Instead, they strained their eyes to see my opponent who was across the field. I glanced across the dusty ground to see Lord Stanton prancing his destrier. The spectators cheered as he went by and women threw scarves and blew kisses at him. Pretending not to notice, William kept his eyes forward and his body perfectly still.

Passing the Queen of Love and Beauty, I gazed up at her. She truly is beautiful, I thought. If only she would wave and smile at me as she had done to the other knights. She didn't. She was talking to an acquaintance and pointing at William across the lists.

Feeling sorry for myself, I sighed and wished Meranda was there to see me. I pictured her face in my mind. She was fairer than the Queen of Love and Beauty and she had loved me, she had told me so. I smiled and held my head up high. I imagined she was watching me and that I wore her ribbon on my helmet.

After circling the field I stopped and steered my horse toward the far end of the lists. As a squire handed me a lance, my eyes caught something moving high up in the stands. It was a man waving his arms and though it was a great distance away, it appeared to be Donovan. Yes, it was he. I waved to him and he jumped up gesticulating. It felt good knowing that at least one person was cheering for me.

A moment later, the marshal and his heralds took their places and before I knew it, the trumpets blared signaling the start of the tilt. I gazed far ahead of me at Lord Stanton and I saw him dig his spurs deep into his steed's flanks. With a cry of excitement he came speeding toward me.

Looking foolish, I did nothing but stare at him. Then, realizing I wasn't moving, I screamed at the top of my lungs and spurred my horse. At first the beast flinched from the quick strike, but soon we were moving along as swiftly as his rippling muscles could carry us. With each galloping stride of the great animals legs, it seemed I went faster and faster than I'd ever gone before. The crowd of faces who watched on either side quickly faded into a blur. The only clear picture I had was of Lord Stanton coming at me with his lance ready to strike.

I leaned forward with my legs clamped around my steed and my feet firmly planted in the stirrups. Preparing for the arriving blow, I lowered my lance and aimed it squarely at William. There was a loud bang and then a crack as my spear splintered upon his shield. At the same instant, his lance made a dull scraping sound and slid off of my shield causing me no harm. Quickly, I glanced back to see if he was still on his horse and disappointingly he was, nevertheless I had scored the first point.

Smiling brightly as I rode back to the starting position, I glanced up at the crowd expecting them to be cheering and applauding. Instead, I heard nothing except the lone shout from an old man high up in the stands. It was Donovan.

A moment later, after positioning myself for the start of the second tilt, a squire raced up and handed me a fresh lance. "Well done sir!" he exclaimed, "I've never seen a point scored on my lord!"

"Watch this," I said with a wink, "I'm going to knock him on his back this time!"

Then the trumpets blared anew and my spurs dug deep into my steed. We took off and my mind was filled with the image of Meranda's sweet face again. I imagined her cheering, blowing kisses, and throwing her scarf to me as I sped toward Lord Stanton.

I was feeling good and confidence seemed to emanate from me like the sweat that dripped from my brow. I knew I had the skill to knock William from his mount. Hearing the rush of the wind as it passed my ears and the stomping of hoofs as they hit the ground, I felt something magical surge through my body. It was an exhilaration that nothing else in the world had ever given me, not even ale.

An instant later, I was upon Lord Stanton. Leaning forward, I carefully aimed my lance and prepared to strike. I cried out in victory as I felt and saw my spear hit its target. Surely this will jolt him from his saddle. I have won!

Suddenly, I found myself floating in the air with my eyes gazing upward into space. Above me was the blue sky. A few gray wisps of clouds were scattered here and there. I was falling and I felt a perfect peacefulness envelope me, but only for a moment. Before I hit the ground, a torturous pain exploded within my chest. William's lance had found me and it was he, not I, who was the victor.

CHAPTER NINE

When I became conscious, my chest ached with every breath I took and my head pounded like a drum. I had a strange sensation that someone was standing over me. I opened my eyes and there was Donovan leaning over me. To my surprise we were in Lord Stanton's great hall.

"Hey young fellow, you're awake! I knew you'd recover!" he bellowed in my face followed by a broad grin that flashed across his pudgy cheeks. He then turned around and yelled, "He's awake!"

I didn't bother to move my head to see whom he was speaking to, but a moment later, Gwendalyn appeared. In her hand she held a warm wet rag that she used to wipe my forehead.

"How do you feel my boy? You gave us quite a scare," she said as I gazed upon her worn yet pleasant face. "You've been out for a day."

"A whole day?" I questioned as the pounding in my head continued.

"Yep, a whole day," answered Donovan still grinning. "You missed the feast, the minstrels, the jugglers, and everything. Don't worry though, I'll tell you all about it on our way to London."

"London," I said, suddenly feeling a sense of urgency. "Yes, that's where I'm going and I should have been there a long time ago." I sat up from my straw bed.

"Now hold on young man!" Gwendalyn put her hand on my chest to stop me from getting up and glared at me with an air of concern in her eyes. "You've been knocked out cold for a day. It's not a good idea to start traipsing around like nothing's happened. You need rest."

She turned to Donovan. "And as for you, you're the one who got him in this mess in the first place. You shouldn't be getting him so excited."

"Me? What did I do?" Donovan asked, putting on his most innocent face.

Gwendalyn scowled at him and shook her fist. She appeared as though she might scream, but no words rang from her lips.

"You certainly don't need to worry about the lad. He's young and he'll bounce back like a cat!" exclaimed Donovan before turning toward me again. "You did good yesterday. You just got a little too confident—that's all. You'll do better next time."

"What kind of ideas are you putting into that boy's head?" Gwendalyn shouted. "He needs to rest! Now go bother someone else before I call my lord and he has you locked up in the dungeon again!"

"Oh, you wouldn't do that now would you?" asked Donovan with a boyish grin on his face.

"Course I would, now scat!"

Donovan winked at me and said, "I'll see you later Winston, that is, when the devil isn't near your bed."

"Oh shush, you filthy man!" cried Gwendalyn as she chased Donovan out of the great hall waving a broomstick in her hands.

"Don't get into trouble!" I yelled after him. "I'm not bailing you out anymore!"

He answered me with only his laughter, which echoed off of the cold stonewalls and then faded away.

For the rest of that day, as I went in and out of sleep, Gwendalyn fed me food which was left over from the prior evening's feast. Lord Stanton came to see me in the evening and he told me I had acted bravely in the tilt against him the day before. He said he was proud of me and that no one had ever scored a point on him before. I fell asleep again and when I awoke, the sun was rising to a new day.

As my eyes opened, the sights, sounds, and smells of breakfast being prepared filled the air. I stretched myself out like a beast after a long winter's nap and wiped the sleep from my eyes. I still was a bit stiff and sore, but I felt much better than the previous day and I knew it was time for me to finally be on my way.

After saying my morning prayers and washing myself, I sat down to a large table in the great hall to eat. There were no lower tables set and Lord Stanton greeted me warmly as did all his knights. Donovan was also seated at the table with a sweeping smile across his face.

"So my lad," said William, "I take it you're ready to go?"

I nodded.

"Well then, I won't keep you any longer. You're free to leave, along with your friend here." He gestured toward Donovan.

Then, with a sullen expression on his face he spoke again. "We will miss you—I will miss you. You have kept yourself as a chivalrous gentleman should." Everyone at the table nodded in agreement. "For that, you have my friendship forever and if there is ever anything I can do for you, just ask."

"I don't know what to say," I replied, feeling overwhelmed. "Thank you."

"No, there is no need to thank me. Now let's eat and when we're done, you'll be fitted with two able horses and given supplies."

"May I sir," Donovan butted in.

Lord Stanton nodded.

"I'd like to propose a toast to Winston. First of all, for staying and helping a foolish fellow who got into trouble when he should have known better. And second, for being a true friend." Donovan looked at me with the most serious expression I had ever seen him wear. "I'm indebted to you and someday I shall repay you."

"Here, here," spoke Sir Richard, as he raised his mug of ale. "I'll drink to that!"

Everyone raised their mugs and clanked them against each other's. Then all eyes fell upon me.

William spoke. "Will you not join us, just this once, with a sip of ale? After all, we're toasting in your honor."

I gazed around the table and saw the calling eyes of every man. The room became hushed and time stood still. They don't understand, I thought. Only those who have been through what I have truly know how it feels. But how can I refuse them when they're rejoicing for me? Maybe I can drink to just one toast.

Without thinking, my hand reached out to an empty mug and a cheerful expression crossed the face of every man in the room. A servant, who had stood silently by with a tankard of ale, quickly bent over and filled my mug. I stared at the amber liquid for a moment and then lifted it to my lips.

Suddenly and fortunately, the remembrance of Emery again entered my mind and before I was even conscious of the act, my hand had turned the mug upside down and slammed it to the table. Ale splashed everywhere and the servant who had poured the brew glared at me annoyingly.

Peering around the table, I saw everyone's mouths open in astonishment and gasps enveloped the room. "I'm sorry!" I protested in my own self-defense to the scowling eyes upon me. "It's nothing against you men! I wouldn't lift a cup of ale for the king! I'm a drinkwater and I pray to God that I shall always be!"

I set my eyes upon the glaring servant and turned my mug right side up again. "Water!" I barked. My tone of voice must have frightened the man for he dashed into the pantry and quickly returned with a pail of water. He filled my mug and I lifted it high into the air. "A toast!" I exclaimed.

Donovan and all the knights looked intently at Lord Stanton to see what he would do. William fixed his eyes upon me with a grave expression. Then slowly, like the cracks that form in drying mud, small clefts appeared at the corners of William's mouth and a moment later they split wide open into a huge smile. "A toast," he shouted, "to Winston!"

A feeling of relief flowed through my mind and a loud cheer, which was led by Donovan, filled the room. "To Winston, the Drinkwater!" I clanked mugs with everyone seated at the table and then I gulped down the sweet tasting water.

After breakfast, we were hasty in our departure for I felt a necessity to be on our way. As Lord Stanton had promised, there were two horses ready for us to take on our journey. Both were brindle in color, and although they were not magnificent beasts, they were fine healthy animals.

To my surprise, William gave me the old armor that I had used in the tilt. "It's not new and shiny, but it will do fine in battle," he said.

I loaded the armor onto my horse and Sir David handed me a bag of bread and dried meat. "I know London is but a day's ride, but it's always good to travel with a full stomach."

"Thank you." I replied.

"We wish you well Winston," quacked Sir John.

Donovan and I mounted our horses and Lord Stanton spoke. "I've got a bit of fine wine imported from the east." He paused and Donovan's eyes lit up for a moment. "I would have given you a jug," he continued with a wink in my direction, "but I know you wouldn't take it, and he," gesturing toward Donovan, "would do better without it." Donovan frowned. "Instead, I give you this jug of spring water. Save it for when you're in London. If you drink the water there you'll become ill."

I extended my hand and took the jug from William. "Thank you for the horses, the armor, and the food. I won't forget you."

"I hope not," replied William. "I understand what lies ahead for you, my son, and I know you must do it on your own terms. But when you're done come visit us, or if beforehand you have any need to call on us, I insist you must. My men and I will come to your aid in a moments notice."

"I know," I replied, shaking his hand firmly. William's dark eyes appeared misty and I too felt a bit of sadness for having to leave his estate. I could say no more though, for I had to be on my way. I waved to the knights and said, "Thank you all." Then I turned my horse around, spurred its flanks, and trotted away.

Donovan followed behind me for a few minutes before he gained complete control of his steed. When he had, he rode up beside me and asked, "What was that all about...'you must do it on your own terms'...and all of that?"

"If you insist on knowing, I shall tell you, though I'm not so sure I should. You mustn't tell anyone of what I say, and since I helped to get you out of that dungeon, you owe me your trust."

"Yes Winston, I know what you're thinking. It's true I'm not the most reliable man, but on my word, I promise to tell not a soul. You're the kindest friend I've ever had and the only one in many years. No one has ever done what you did for me. I didn't expect you to stay and help me and when you did, I was surprised. For that I am grateful."

Donovan rarely spoke in such an earnest manner and it really touched me. Because of this, I went on to tell him about everything that had happened to me in the last eight months.

"Ah, it's as I thought. You are from a noble home. That's where you learned your skill with the sword."

"No!" I replied, nearly yelling at him. "I learned from an experienced master, a great and caring man, whose death was brought about by my own selfish want for ale and by the foulness of a snake named Cyrus!"

"Okay, I didn't mean anything by it," replied Donovan, becoming quiet and sullen.

Leaving Hertford behind us we passed over a bridge above a shallow stream where local women were doing their wash. It was a warm summer day and London was less than twenty miles away. We would be there in four hours or less if we didn't stop for anything and if the horses didn't become too hot.

Numerous travelers passed us along the road and we greeted them with pleasant hellos. Most were peasants, probably on errands for their masters, dressed in cloudy gray tunics. A few were attired in bright colors, nobleman or merchants I presumed. The majority of the latter ignored us and our friendly greetings.

I recalled the last time I had traveled a country road and how the three highwaymen had tried to rob me. I reached down and felt the leather covered hilt of the sword that Emery had given me. Knowing it was at my side reassured me, though it was unlikely I would have to make use of it. Bandits preferred empty roads with plenty of places to hide where they could ambush a lone party. The road we traveled was well used and gave little chance for a robber to ply his trade.

"So you plan on avenging your father by killing this man Cyrus?" Donovan asked me.

"Yes, I must. What else can I do?"

"You could leave it alone and not do anything—just live your life and forget about it."

"That would be a cowardly thing to do. And even if I did, what would I do with myself, become a poor peddler like you?"

"Well—I thought we could travel around England together, you know, sort of a partnership." Donovan smiled and his pudgy cheeks shone with life.

I wanted to laugh out loud, but I could tell the foolish peddler was being serious. I didn't want to hurt his feelings so I just smiled and said, "I'm sorry Donovan, but I must do what—"

"—I have to do. I know," he replied, "it was just a thought. Instead, I will go with you and help you kill this evil man."

"You? What can you do but get in my way or cause more trouble than I already have?"

"You shall see I'm not as worthless as you might think."

I chuckled. "You may come, but if you cause even one problem, you're on your own."

"Agreed. Now tell me of your plan."

As we went on our way, I told Donovan why I was going to London to find my good friend Eric. I explained how, with Eric's help and the help of his father's men, I'd be able to get close enough to fight and kill Cyrus myself.

"It's that simple?" asked Donovan.

"Yes," I replied, "it is."

"Well then, why didn't you ask Lord Stanton for his help when he offered it?"

"I thought about it, but it's not his fight. Besides, he only has seven knights. What good would they be against thirty of forty rogues? I'm sure Cyrus has hired at least that many to help him control Dereham."

"Lord Stanton could have obtained more men than that in a day! You saw how the gentry at the tournament respected him. With one word he could get a hundred men."

"I'm not so sure," I replied, "and besides, as I said before, it's not his fight."

"Well what makes it Eric's fight? Could it be that you're reluctant to come face to face with Cyrus? Maybe you know that searching for Eric will bide you more time before you must confront the man."

"No!" I shouted in a rage, knowing that Donovan was implying that I was afraid. "Don't you ever say that!" I grabbed him by the collar and threw him down hard from off of his horse.

With his hands out to stop him, Donovan hit the earth with a thud and he stayed there for a moment not moving. Then quietly he rolled up onto his knees and began wiping the dirt from his clothes. He would not look at me. His palms were bleeding and by the expression on his face, so were his feelings.

I didn't blame him for being upset. I shouldn't have become so enraged. Maybe he was right, I considered. Maybe all the time I had spent in Hertford had been an unconscious underlying plan by myself to delay facing Cyrus Everett. After all, the corpulent pig of a man had brought me to death's door once already. Why would I not be afraid of facing him again? No, it couldn't be so I told myself, and I pushed the notion from my mind. Still, I shouldn't have been so rough on my peddler friend.

"I'm sorry," I said, reaching my hand out to help Donovan back on his horse. He wouldn't accept it and he struggled onto the beast by himself. Somberly, we continued on together, though the rest of the day's journey was a quiet one.

*　　*　　*

It was early afternoon when we arrived upon the marshy outskirts of northern London. We could see the great wall that had been built by the Romans stretching out before us in the distance. The barrier surrounded much of London and was quite useful in earlier times against Viking raiders. Tiny shacks dotted the landscape and as we came closer to the city, these dwellings appeared more frequently. Peasants worked the lush green fields and as I gazed about the countryside, I inhaled deeply and smelled the sharp aroma of freshly cut grass.

I didn't know what to expect of the great city for I had never been there. I knew from my schooling that all or parts of the city had been burned down many times during the last few centuries. Consistently, after the fires were put out, the citizens would quickly rebuild and again they would use wood. It was too costly for anyone but the very wealthy to build with stone or brick. Thus, the city was forever vulnerable to catastrophic fires.

As we came upon the huge gate at the northern entrance, Donovan and I said nothing; we just stared in wonder. The gate itself, being old and rusty, was left open and probably hadn't been used in years. We entered.

Gazing about the streets, I noticed them to be covered with filth and garbage. That, in combination with the warm sun, had caused an overwhelming stench that burned my nostrils as I inhaled. It was hard to imagine how people could live in such a place. The lanes were narrow and the second stories of most buildings jutted out over the streets nearly blocking out all of the sunlight. No wonder fire spread so quickly here, I thought.

Though filth ridden, the streets were not empty. They were crowded with people hurrying here and there, pushing carts or leading horses. Most of them rushed by in haste with grimaces on their faces. Few looked anyone in the eye, for fear it seemed, that they might have to acknowledge another's existence and thus be personable. No one seemed to care who we were or what we were doing, except a number of peddlers trying to sell us their useless gadgets or miracle cures.

Remembering the last letter I had received from Eric, I recalled that he was spending his time in a place called Dowgate where the wharfs were located. I asked a sullen appearing man, dressed in the manner of a merchant, if he knew of the place. Pleasantly enough, he pointed me in the direction.

As the two of us traveled over the rough and muddled streets, we passed a poor man being pulled around in a cart with his hands tied behind his back. He was naked except for two loaves of bread strapped to his chest and a sign on his back that stated, 'This is what ye receive for selling sand in your flour'. Justice, I presumed, for a dishonest miller.

As we were about to round a corner, Donovan finally spoke to me again, "Stop! Do you hear that?"

I listened and heard a clapping noise. "What is it?"

"A leper!" he exclaimed. "Let's take another street!"

We turned our horses and headed back from where we had come. A moment later, I glanced behind me and saw a grossly disfigured man clapping two pieces of wood together as he walked. He was rounding the corner of the lane where we had almost entered. His face was so hideous I shuddered.

"They're supposed to stay in their own part of the city," said Donovan, "but they go wherever they like."

"Why is that?" I asked.

"If you were the sheriff or county steward, would you want to arrest one of them?"

"I see," I said, directing my horse down a side street. "Come Donovan, this way."

After escaping the leper, we trotted along the city streets for about a quarter hour before the smell of fish entered my nose. A few minutes later, we were passing the wharfs along Fishmonger's Street. In front of us, the river Thames was spread out like an enormous winding serpent. It seemed wondrously alive with the afternoon sun reflecting off of its rippling waves. Woman and children dotted the shoreline, while men in boats were out on its great waters fishing and sailing.

"Enchanting, isn't it?" asked Donovan, with a simple smile on his face.

"Yes," I replied, for I too was mesmerized by the great shimmering river, "but we can't stay here all day. We must find a place to bed for the night."

A half hour later, we found an inn on Brecon Street, two blocks up from the docks. It wasn't in the best part of town, but it was as close to Dowgate and the wharfs as we could find. The innkeeper charged us a small fortune for our own room, but it was better than sharing one with half a dozen scruffy looking rogues. I had heard too many tales of travelers whose throats had been slit and their belongings taken after sharing a room at a London inn.

Our quarters were located on the second floor and as we made our way up to our room we were propositioned by three quite attractive strumpets. I declined their offers and Donovan did so regretfully with my urging. From the sounds we heard coming through the paper thin doors, we concluded that the three proposals we had encountered were not merely isolated incidents.

The lower story of the inn was an alehouse and it had its charm, including a cozy fireplace surrounded by wooden tables and chairs. The only drawback was that many of the men sitting at those tables and resting on those chairs appeared to be ruffians and cutthroats.

After inspecting our room, Donovan convinced me to sit with him for a moment so that he could have a mug of ale. We found a table next to the hissing fire and took a seat.

"Ale!" yelled Donovan to the brewer.

"Two?" questioned the heavy man.

"No, just one," replied Donovan.

"What'll you have?" the brewer asked me with an expectant glare.

I studied the man for a moment. He was fat and disgusting in appearance. Droplets of sweat crowned his bald head and shimmered vividly in the flickering light of the fire. He reminded me of Cyrus Everett. Since I had left the fresh jug of spring water, which Lord Stanton had given me, up in our room, I asked, "Do you have any fresh water?"

The fat man cackled, as did many of the other patrons in the tavern. "If you want water, you can get it out of the gutter outside!"

This comment brought more laughter from the crowd around us. My face and neck flushed hot with anger, but I held my tongue. The last thing I wanted was to draw even more attention to Donovan and I.

"That was a rude thing for him to say," whispered Donovan.

"Yes," I agreed, "but let's not make a scene. Just drink your ale and keep quiet."

"Okay, okay, but I haven't said anything," replied Donovan with a sheepish expression.

"I know," I said, "but I'm just worried that you might."

Just then the brewer returned with a mug of ale and I paid him his penny. Donovan gulped down the liquid and called for more. By the time he was on his fifth, his cheeks were rosy and he had a continuous smile on his face.

"Well now," Donovan jabbered, "what do we do now? Where will we find this friend of yours?"

"I'm not sure, but if we scour this part of the city for a few days I'm sure we'll come upon him."

"And you're sure he'll help you?"

"Yes, I'm sure. He was my father's squire and now he's a knight."

"What does a knight do in the city?"

"Truly I don't know, except that his father deals with many of the merchants in London. I think he has Eric keep an eye on things for him."

While we spoke, two men entered the tavern. I paid no particular attention to them as they greeted a number of patrons and bought themselves some ale. Then they came to our table and stood in front of it. After ignoring them for a moment, I finally glanced up to see what they wanted.

What I saw was a man, probably in his fourth decade of life, with a lengthy scraggly beard and a few missing teeth. He was tall with a lean muscular build. Beside him stood a short stocky fellow with a bald head.

"That be our table there!" The bearded man growled.

I looked the man in the eyes for a moment to get a sense of who he was and what he wanted. He didn't look away. I could smell his wretched breath and it was strong with the stench of drink. I probably should have moved to another table to appease the ruffian. However, I was still feeling hot from the boorish comment made earlier by the brewer, so instead I spoke up. "There are many tables open. You may sit at any of them or, if you'd like, you may join us at this one."

"I don't think you understand lad! That's my table and I don't plan on sharing it with a dog like you!"

At that instant, Donovan stood up and moved to the next table.

"I think your friend there has the right idea!" snarled the bearded man. "And if you're as smart as he is you'll do the same!"

The room became quiet and all eyes were upon me. I glanced over at Donovan and he was motioning me to come sit with him. I should have followed his guidance, but unfortunately my anger had risen beyond control from the degrading comments being spewed by the blackguard who stood before me. I glared at the two ruffians. "Why should I?" I asked.

The two brutes appeared astonished. I was sure they had pushed around many a stranger and had never before heard a reply like mine. The bearded man's face turned red and his body trembled with rage. The stocky man's skin went pale and he let out a snort like some strange beast.

"Cause I'll cut out your tongue and feed it to the rats if you don't shut your mouth and move!" barked the furious man.

"Okay," I said, deliberately standing abruptly to see how the two hooligans would react. They backed away quickly and stumbled over each other's feet.

"Alright, that's it! I've had enough out of you!" yelled the bearded rogue as he came at me bearing all his weight behind his right fist.

I stepped to my left and ducked. His fist grazed the top of my head and as it went past I grabbed it with both hands and pulled. He rolled head over heels upon the tabletop and then crashed to the floor nearly landing in the crackling fire.

Appearing frightened, but knowing he would be shamed if he didn't help his friend, the short stocky man swung at me. I blocked his blow with my left forearm and punched him squarely in the face with my right hand. He stumbled backwards, dancing on his feet like a court jester. Then, hearing a noise, I turned around just in time to face the bearded man who had recovered from his fall.

"Now you shall surely die!" he bellowed, pulling his sword from his sheath.

I drew my sword also, and readied myself for the attack. As I had presumed, the man was used to employing his great physical strength to overpower his foes, and he came straight at me. He had no idea that I would use his own great strength against him, as Emery had taught me. He jabbed at my torso and as he did, I stepped again to my left and kicked out my right foot. Tripping over it, the rogue fell flat on the floor and a round of laughter echoed through the tavern.

I gazed around and prepared myself for another attack from the stocky bald man, but he had already given up. He was resting on the floor with his back against the wall while holding his nose, which bled profusely.

I glanced at Donovan and he was still seated at his table but now he was laughing with drink in hand. Suddenly, he motioned toward the floor behind me. The sword-yielding rapscallion was regaining his stance and readying himself for a third attack.

"Come now McCracken, is that the best you have to offer the lad?" shouted a patron in the room.

"You'll be next," muttered the ruffian as he fully rose to his feet.

"Sir," I said, regaining some of my self-control, "wouldn't it be wise to stop this foolishness and sit down like gentleman?"

"The only fool here is you," he replied, "and soon you'll be dead!"

Obviously the man was still in no mood to talk things over. He came at me again, but this time he attacked more slowly, slicing his blade back and forth. It was clear to me that he wasn't a skilled swordsman.

As he advanced, I held out my blade firmly and caught his sword with mine. I began spinning my blade around and around and when I saw the chance, I quickly thrust forward, cutting his hand and loosening his grip. Then, I caught the hilt of his sword with the tip of my blade and with a quick flick of my wrist his blade went flying across the room. Everyone in its path ducked, so as not to be pierced by it, and it came to rest firmly in the far wall. The crowd erupted with cheer.

I was genuinely amazed with myself. I had no idea that the few months I'd spent with Emery had prepared me so well. It was true that the man before me was not a well-trained knight, but he was husky and powerful, yet I was handling him like a baby kitten. I had little time to congratulate myself though, for he came at me again.

"Arrgh!" he growled, running full tilt at me.

Setting my sword down on a nearby table, I planted my left leg firmly behind me and placed my right leg forward lightly on the floor. When he almost reached me, I stepped to the right and spun my body full circle so that just as he passed, I was behind him. I kicked him in the rear with all my whirling energy and he went flying into the wall headfirst. The crowd cheered again and cackles and guffaws filled the air. I picked up my sword from off of the table where I'd left it and placed it in its sheath.

The bearded man lay on the floor and moved his arms for a moment as if to get up, but then he let out a moan and collapsed face down. He was either unconscious or just too tired to fight anymore. The patrons in the alehouse were still clapping and cheering when I heard a strange but familiar voice.

"Good show Winston, good show!"

I turned toward the voice and there, standing by the front door of the tavern, stood Eric Braden. That is, he had the face of my old friend Eric, but his body was completely different than the youth I remembered from only a year or so ago. Eric had always been tall, but rather skinny. The man who stood before me was also tall, but his chest was huge and his arms resembled limbs on a tree. Could this be the same Eric? I wondered.

I gazed at him. His eyes were a brilliant green and placed between them was a modest delicate nose. Below that, was a grinning dainty mouth encircled by a square powerful jaw. It was him all right, everything was there including the black curly locks surrounding his face.

"Winston!" he yelled. "Lord, it's good to see you!" He reached out his hand and shook mine. "Ah, forget the handshake," he said, wrapping his huge arms around me and nearly squeezing the wind out of me. "I thought you might be dead my friend. Where have you been?

And look at you—you're so lean and strong. The last time I saw you, you were beginning to get—well—sort of portly."

"Well look at you," I replied. "When did you replace your body with a tree trunk?"

He laughed vigorously and asked, "Where did you learn to fight like that? I've never seen anything like it."

"Do you remember the old hermit who lived in the Staverton Forest?"

"You mean the crazy recluse who lived alone in the woods? What about him?"

"His name was Emery and he was a great swordsman. He's the one who taught me."

"That's hard to believe," replied Eric, "but if you say it's so, than I know it's the truth. Come, sit down." We sat at the table where Donovan and I had originally been seated.

"Donovan, come over here!" I called. He ambled over with a mammoth grin on his face and I introduced him to Eric and the two shook hands.

There was another man with Eric whom he introduced as George. "This is my bailiff and counselor, a trustworthy man. He's always with me wherever I go, especially when it has to do with business."

George was a bit heavy and at least ten years older than Eric. He had a pleasant face and appeared genuinely happy to meet me. "I've heard much about you and your family," he said.

"I see you've already met Ralph McCracken." Eric gestured to the man lying on the floor.

"You know him?"

"Yes, he's a bit stubborn and bullheaded, and he loves to fight, but really he's quite loyal."

I gazed at the poor man on the floor who appeared to be waking from a long nap. "Eric, I never thought you would consort with a man the likes of him."

"Oh, he's just a little rough around the edges, that's all. He's been on my side and stood up for me in many a brawl."

"And who's that?" I asked, pointing to the stocky bald man who was still holding his nose.

"That's Peter Cook, not the greatest fighter you've ever met, but he's a good blacksmith when he's not drunk." Turning to the two injured men, Eric called, "Peter! Ralph! Come over here and meet my friend! This is Winston Tabor. I was first a page and then a squire to his father."

Ralph McCracken stood slowly, growled slightly, and nodded. He ambled over and perched himself grudgingly on the edge of a chair across the table from me.

Peter came forward gazing at me timidly and said, "Sorry sir, we didn't mean to cause you any trouble." At that, McCracken glared at him. Peter frowned and then rested himself in a chair.

"Alright," Eric spoke up in a serious tone. "Enough with the introductions. Winston, I'm greatly saddened by the death of your parents. I just learned about it yesterday when we returned to my father's estate in Bremley. You see my father and I have been on the mainland in France attempting to work out a venture to import wine. While we were away, my mother had received a letter from Shelby."

"Shelby? You've heard from him? What did he say?"

"Let me finish and you'll find out."

I nodded and Eric continued. "Shelby wrote this letter addressed to my father. My mother, being a proper lady and feeling that the letter was personal, didn't open it. When we arrived yesterday my father read it. If we had only known sooner, we would have come to your aid."

"I know you would have," I said. "Is Shelby still in Dereham under the rule of that wicked Cyrus?"

"No he isn't and this is how I know. Along with that letter there was a second more recent letter that my mother had received just two days ago. It said that Shelby was on his way to Bremley with a heavy heart. It seems that Cyrus has been mistreating the village people and has taxed them heavily. Shelby attempted to stay on with Cyrus even after the terrible death of your mother, so that when you returned to punish him for his crimes you would have someone on the inside to help you. Finally though, the letter stated that he had had to leave, for he wasn't sure if you were still alive. Also, it seems that the townsfolk, Shelby's true friends, were beginning to look down on him with disfavor."

"I see," I said. "Shelby has always been a good man. It must have hurt him so to pretend to be loyal to Cyrus."

"Yes," agreed Eric. "So I came here to Dowgate knowing that this was the last place I told you I was staying. I thought, just maybe, you would be here searching for me and it seems that luck was on my side. Shelby should arrive any day now at my father's estate and we'll be able to talk to him first hand about the developments unfolding in Dereham."

"Yes, that will be quite valuable. Then I can think of the best way to avenge my father and mother."

Eric nodded. "Once we know how many cutthroats Cyrus has under his command, we'll gather an appropriate number of fighting men and journey to Dereham."

"I knew if anyone could help me, it would be you Eric."

Eric smiled and raised his mug of ale. "A toast to Winston and to the death of Cyrus!"

Everyone lifted their mugs and drank except for me. Eric eyed me with a questioning glare. "Why is it that you're not drinking?" he asked.

Donovan interrupted, "Don't you know? The lad's a drinkwater."

Eric scratched his head, pondering for a moment. "How did this come to be Winston? From what I recall, you were uh, well, you had grown quite fond of ale if you don't mind me saying so."

"Too fond," I replied, adding no further explanation.

"I understand," said Eric with a sympathetic expression on his face.

I was glad that Eric understood why I was not drinking. It was a relief to not have to explain to a crowd of men, yet again, why I had quitted the drink.

"How long have you been in town?" Eric asked.

"We just arrived today."

"Where have you been all this time before coming to London and how is it that you were blamed for your father's death and not Cyrus?"

I explained to Eric and all the men at the table how Cyrus had framed me for the murder of my father. I described my time spent with Emery. I told them also of how I met Donovan on my journey to London and how I help saved him from imprisonment by befriending Lord Stanton.

Then, as the rest of the men drank, Eric and I talked more about what had happened to me and also about our plans for the coming days. I explained how my drunkenness had led to the death of Emery. I told him of the beautiful girl I had met and fallen in love with and how I hoped to one day see her again. He told me about the work he did for his father and how he was worried about his father's health. We reminisced of old times, laughing and joking until late into the night.

One thing kept bothering me throughout our discussion however. It seemed to me that Ralph McCracken continually glared at me with a dreadful scowl. I almost said something to him, but then I decided to shrug it off. What did I expect from a man whom I had made a fool of in front of his cohorts?

Eventually, our gathering grew weary as the night wore on and we decided to retire. We agreed that in the morning we would all leave for Bremley and await Shelby's arrival.

*   *   *

It was late morning by the time Donovan and I had woke, dressed, and left our room. As we stepped outside, I noticed the sun was just beginning to break through the smoky haze that enveloped the gray shrouded city. We strolled to the stable at the back of the inn where our horses had been bedded for the night. The stable master assured us that the animals had been fed and watered properly, so I paid the man and Donovan and I loaded our supplies and mounted our horses. We rode them back around to Brecon Street to await Eric and his men.

"Tis a fine morning for July," said Donovan.

"That it is," I agreed.

"Winston, what do you think of that McCracken fellow? I don't like the looks of him."

I laughed. "I don't care too much for him either, but we've met him only once. First encounters can be deceiving. Eric has always been a good judge of character and if he trusts him than so shall we."

"Alright, but I still don't like him."

"I never said you had to like him, just give him a chance, that's all."

Donovan frowned, but he nodded in agreement. A moment later we heard the sound of horse's hoofs trotting upon the hard stamped earth. It was Eric and his three companions, George, Peter, and Ralph McCracken.

We greeted them and surprisingly even Ralph nodded his head to acknowledge me when I said good morning. We conversed for a few moments and everyone seemed to be in good spirits. A minute later we were on our way to Bremley with a warm wind at our backs.

As we traveled, the day became brighter and I was delighted with having the opportunity to view the filthy yet fascinating city of London further. We passed a wharf where peddlers sold fish and sailors were unloading tankards of wine from a large sailing ship. Further on, we went by a public cooking house and my mouth watered as the smell of sizzling meat crossed paths with my nose. Traveling by the crowded and noisy guildsmen's shops, we stopped for a moment to watch the skilled craftsmen as they went about their daily work. Everyone we saw we greeted with a smile and hello. Some received us in the same manner, but most glared at us suspiciously or ignored us completely as was the custom, I had recently learned, in such a big city.

Coming to the edge of town, the air smelled fresher and the sky was less hazy. Eric asked me where we had gotten our horses and how I had come upon such a strange looking sword.

I informed him more about the old man Emery, how I had received his sword, and where it was originally from. I described the skills the old man had taught me. Also, I told Eric further of my adventures with Lord Stanton and his knights and how he had given us the horses for our travels.

Eric was quite amazed at everything I had been through and he told me he was genuinely happy that I no longer partook in drink. He said I looked better and seemed more happy and confident than ever before.

When I thought about it, I realized he was right. Though I was saddened by my parent's deaths and all the terrible things Cyrus had done, I truly was a happier man. For the first time in my life I really knew who I was and what I stood for. Nothing controlled my spirit but me. I was as free as a mortal man could hope to be.

Our ride went by quickly, and before we knew it, we were in sight of Lord Braden's estate. It was a capacious stone manor with a deep moat around it. Long narrow fields of wheat and barley surrounded the moat. The drawbridge was down and, as we crossed it and entered the open gates, a servant greeted us.

Then suddenly, a woman with a familiar face came dashing out of the main keep and ran up to us. Her skin was aged and worn, though her appearance was still agreeable. She wore an elegant kirtle and her hair was tied up in plaits and covered with a coif. "Eric!" she called.

"Yes mother?"

Of course, I marveled, she is Eric's mother, Elizabeth. I hadn't seen her since I was a child. She was always as sweet to me as my own mother and my memories of her were filled with fondness.

"Shelby's here," she said, "but not with Winston. He hasn't heard a word from him since Lord Tabor's death and he fears the worst. He's sick with sadness for all he's seen and gone through. I don't want to break his heart, but it seems to me that if you've not heard from Winston either, than we must presume the worst."

"Mother!" Eric exclaimed, motioning his arm toward me.

"Oh, I'm sorry," she said. "Where are my manners? You've not introduced me."

I leaped off of my horse and hastened up to her. Stretching my arms out, I prepared to embrace her.

"Aack! What are you doing?" cried Eric's mother.

Our troupe erupted with laughter and Elizabeth appeared confused. She quickly gazed at Eric for reassurance.

I stepped back and said, "I was trying to greet you. Don't you remember me?"

Elizabeth stared at me for a moment and then took a step closer. "Winston? Is that you?"

"Yes, it's me!"

"Why—I guess it is you. You've grown into quite a man." She took me into her arms and kissed me on the cheek. Tears of joy fell from her eyes and she sobbed. "Oh it's so good to know you're alright. We've been so worried." Then she released me and turned to her son. "Eric, why didn't you tell me you had found Winston before I made a fool of myself in front of everyone?"

"You didn't give me a chance mother," he replied chuckling.

A moment later, after introducing Donovan to his mother, Eric suggested that we all go in and talk to Shelby. Eric had Ralph and Peter stable the horses while the rest of us strode across the small courtyard and entered the main hall.

Once inside the huge room, I noticed a fire dancing in the center of a great stone hearth. Its smoke twirled up to the ceiling and found its way out through a round hole in the roof. Three tables were set and all were empty except for the highest where a thin tired looking man was seated. It was Shelby.

CHAPTER TEN

Shelby caught a glimpse of me and a smile quickly emerged on his face. His tired appearance was washed away and replaced with the look of a man twenty years younger. He quickly stood up and I rushed over to him.

"Winston, your alive!" he exclaimed as he shook my hand and then embraced me.

"Of course, did you think I was not?"

"I didn't know what to think," he replied with delight beaming from his green misting eyes. "I knew only that you narrowly escaped death on your first bout with Cyrus and that you must have evaded it again at the old hermit's cottage. Since then I've heard nothing."

"Well here I am in flesh and blood," I said smiling.

"Yes, and I thank God for that," replied Shelby grinning. "I thought something awful had happened to you. Even Cyrus wonders where you've gone. He's afraid you're still alive and that you're planning vengeance."

"That I am!"

Suddenly our greeting was interrupted by a voice that sounded as deep as the sea. "Please, sit down everyone."

I turned and there standing before me was Eric's father, Lord Braden. He was a tall man, well built and powerful. He was the sort of man whose presence commanded respect and when he spoke everyone listened.

"You're my guests and you must be hungry. Sit and let us be served."

"Lord Braden," I said, "I apologize for not greeting you, but I was so caught up with seeing Shelby that I—"

"There's no need for apologies my son," his voice thundered, "and please call me Harold as you had as a young boy."

"Yes sir," I replied with great reverence.

"It is truly good to see you Winston. It quiets my heart to know you're alright."

"Thank you. I'm glad to be with you and your family again. It reminds me of being home."

"I'm glad you feel that way," he said, "but may I ask why you didn't come to us at the beginning? You know we would always help you, don't you?"

"Yes," I replied, "it's a long story and you shall hear it soon enough."

Harold smiled and nodded. "I understand. Now who is this friend of yours?"

I introduced Donovan and afterward we were seated at the high table. Just then Ralph McCracken and Peter the blacksmith entered the hall. They greeted Lord Braden and sat down at the middle table. McCracken glared at me with an air of contempt as if I didn't belong at the high table. I ignored him.

As the servants prepared our food, I explained to Shelby and Lord Braden what had happened to me since my father's murder. They both listened intently.

While speaking, a servant came around the table pouring ale for everyone. Though the temptation was there, I refused it kindly and asked for water.

Shelby appeared amazed when he saw that I had asked for water and he questioned me. I told him and Lord Braden how and why I had become a drinkwater and how much happier I was. Surprisingly, neither of them looked strangely at me or questioned me further after I told my story. Instead, they were glad for me and very proud. Shelby added that the drink would have eventually led to the death of me. It nearly had.

When I was done speaking, the food was ready and our trenchers were laid out before us to eat off of. The servants began serving the meat and there was plenty of it; bacon, veal, fish, and poultry, along with bowls of spicy sauces to dip it into. The table was also covered with ripe cherries, peaches, raspberries, and plums. There were bowls of peas, leeks, turnips, and onions. It was a grand meal.

I picked up a peach and took a bite. Its juice squirted out between my lips and rolled down my chin onto my tunic. It was so sweet and delicious that I finished it off with just two more bites. Then I picked up a piece of veal and dipped it into a bowl of peppery sauce. Its flavor exploded upon my tongue.

"I'm glad I'm not a monk," said Eric after he finished off a pheasant leg dripping with spicy sauce and tossed the bone to the rush-covered floor.

"Yes indeed," I agreed, knowing that men of the cloth could not enjoy food with such palatable spices. They believed them to be aphrodisiacs.

Gazing around at the table of men, I listened to the sounds of them chewing and gnawing. No one spoke, but pleasure radiated from everyone's face. Even McCracken seemed to be enjoying himself in my presence.

When we were finished, the house servants picked up our trenchers and gave them to the beggars who were waiting outside. The soggy chunks of stale bread were always a welcome sight to the very poor.

I wiped my face with my sleeve and spoke. "Now tell me Shelby, tell me all that has happened since I was forced to flee Dereham."

"First, let me tell you this," he said as he picked a chunk of meat from his teeth and flicked it to the floor. "From the very beginning, I had no intention of being an accomplice with Cyrus. I had to make a decision to either confront the man or pretend that I would be his servant. I decided it would be my undoing to defy him since he controlled everyone and everything. You know how he is."

"Yes Shelby, I do. Now don't blame yourself for anything. You did what you had to and I'm thankful."

"For weeks I tried to speak with your mother, but Cyrus and his hired men would not let me. I could only watch from afar as your mother's grief and innocence was used against her. Before her eyes Cyrus appeared to be the kindest of gentleman, while behind them he planned and conspired a plot to win her love and your father's castle. I'm sorry to say I did nothing, but I never believed for a moment that your mother was in harm's way. Cyrus used her like a tool and when she became useless to him he discarded that tool."

"I heard," I said, "she fell down the stairs?"

"Yes, and Cyrus was the only witness. The townsfolk were suspicious and there was talk of murder, but Cyrus hired more rogues to keep Dereham under control. He paid for the hired men by taxing the village even more heavily than ever."

"That rapscallion!" Eric exclaimed, catching my eyes with his. "I'll enjoy watching you kill him."

"Aye, and I'll enjoy killing him," I replied. Then I asked Shelby to continue his story.

"Well at first, after your duel with Cyrus and after his men went to recover your body and it wasn't there, rumors surfaced that you still might be alive. This made Cyrus shiver in his boots, for he knew if you still lived you would do all you could to avenge your father. He sent men out to search for you daily, but none of them ever came up with anything. I believe he began to think that you were dead and that your body had been devoured by foxes as had part of Hector's corpse."

"The foolish pig!" I growled.

"Then one morning three men arrived from the town of Cawston. They told Cyrus that for a fee they would give him some very interesting information. Cyrus paid them and they told him how as wanderers they often came to Dereham because the town's Lord was known for his kindness. It seems your father, Lord Tabor, always gave them a good meal and a warm place to bed for the night."

Shelby stopped for a moment, coughed, and took a sip of ale. The room was quiet and everyone at the table was waiting for Shelby to continue.

I, of course, knew the unfortunate outcome of the tale being told and I began to feel a bit uncomfortable. However, I decided not to interrupt him. "Please go on," I said.

"Well, these men told Cyrus about a man they had seen the prior evening in Cawston at the village brewer's. They said the man reminded them of Lord Tabor's only son, and they knew he was wanted."

A feeling of shame came over me. I knew the men that Shelby spoke of were the three who had beaten me that terrible night in Cawston when I was drunk. "So that's how they knew who I was," I muttered.

My father, being a kindhearted man, had always fed wayward wanderers. I had never paid much attention to any of them, so I wouldn't have remembered one vagabond from another, but obviously these three men had remembered me. "The scoundrels!" I shouted as anger overcame my feeling of disgrace. "They bit the hand that fed them for a few pennies!"

"Oh, I believe they received their just rewards," said Shelby. "No one ever saw the trio leave Dereham. Cyrus is much too greedy to part from money when he doesn't have too."

I smiled for a moment, but soon my lips twisted into a frown as I again recalled that night in the Tavern. In my drunkenness, I had acted as a fool and it had led to the death of my friend Emery. How could I ever forgive myself for that? Forgetting where I was for a moment, my eyes became misty and my heart filled with sadness.

"Are you alright lad?" Donovan asked, appearing concerned.

"Yes, just a bad memory. That's all," I said. Then I asked Shelby, "How did Cyrus come to find that I was staying with the old man in the forest?"

"After his talk with the three wanderers, Cyrus and his men went to Cawston to question everyone they could. On their way there they met a peasant who rents property from Baron Wellington. The property he rents is upstream and across from where the old hermit lived. He told Cyrus about you. It seems you had visited his cottage a time or two."

"Yes, I know the man. His name's Roger Cayton," I said. Then I thought of his beautiful daughter Meranda and sadness again filled my heart.

Shelby seemed to sense my despondency and asked, "Should I continue?"

"No, I know what happened after that. Just tell me how you ended up here."

"Well, I continued to work as a servant for Cyrus while trying to get word out to you, but there was never any reply. After awhile, the townsfolk began to view me as a villain, so finally I had to leave Dereham. There was never any question in my mind who I would seek out to help me. I knew it would be Lord Braden and his family, but I had trouble finding them. I had no idea at which estate they were lodging and little did I know that Eric and his father were on the mainland in France. Eventually though, I caught up with them and I arrived here last evening."

"You made a wise choice," said Eric's father in his deep voice, "and from here we shall plan Winston's retribution."

All who were in the room smiled and nodded in agreement. All, that is, except for Ralph McCracken who sat silently by grimacing.

"Winston, there's one more thing I might add," spoke Shelby. "It's probably unimportant, but it underlines just how uncaring and disrespectful Cyrus has been toward you and your family, especially your mother."

"What more could he possibly do? He's already murdered both of my parents."

"He plans to marry again, just two months after your mother's death."

"Ah, the man is the devil!" I cried. "His lack of honor makes me wretch! Who is this foul woman?"

"A simple peasant girl."

When Shelby said those words, my heart jumped in my chest and it began beating as fast as the wings on a hummingbird. I was afraid to ask for a name, but before I could speak, Shelby continued.

"She's the daughter of the man who led Cyrus to the old hermit's cottage. I believe her name is Meranda."

Instantly, my bowels felt as though they had been sliced open and were spilling out over the floor. Dizziness came over me and a wave of grief enveloped me. Cyrus had already taken my parents and my home, now he was about to take the only sunlight left in my world.

Shelby proceeded with his story. "Cyrus met her when he was questioning the girl's father about you Winston. Her father gladly agreed to the marriage since Cyrus is now such a wealthy man."

"Winston, are you okay?" asked Eric, placing his hand on my shoulder. "You look rather pale. Do you know this girl?"

"I did," I said, "but it matters no more."

Eric's father broke in. "Shelby, does the girl wish to marry Cyrus?"

"No, I should say not. Cyrus wanted no one to know, but I heard she put up quite a fuss when she found out. I guess she cried for nearly a week."

"When is the wedding?" asked Lord Braden.

"A week from today, next Sunday," replied Shelby.

"Ah my lad," rang Lord Braden's voice, "don't look so sullen. We've got a whole week. It won't take more than two days to round up some men and it's only a three day ride to Dereham at most."

I gazed up at Harold's soft strong face and he reminded me of my own dear father. Quickly, my mood swung to brighter thoughts. Lord Braden's words had just opened the door to so many possibilities. "Really? You would do this for me, and so quickly?"

"Of course. Your father would have done the same for Eric. It's the least I can do for you."

"A peasant girl?" questioned Eric with a broad smile on his face.

I glared at him with an air of annoyance.

"It's alright Winston, you can't help what your heart does to you." Eric put his hand in my hair and roughed it up a bit.

"That's true my son," said Eric's father. "I'll hold no ill will toward you. Beauty is one gift given from God which is shared by all peoples."

I was glad that Eric and Lord Braden felt the way they did, for I had often wondered if there was something wrong with me for caring so much about a peasant girl. They had set my mind at ease and for the rest of that evening I was able to concentrate on the preparation of our strategy to avenge my father and mother.

*   *   *

Two days later, on Tuesday morning, we left Bremley with a party of twenty-six men including Donovan and I.

Lord Braden had taken suddenly ill and although he didn't like the idea, Eric and I convinced him that it would be best if he didn't come along. He was not stricken terribly, but enough so that the trip to Dereham may have made him seriously ill. I directed Shelby to stay with him and to join us only when Lord Braden was feeling his best again.

Our group consisted of Ralph McCracken, Peter the blacksmith, George, Eric, Donovan and I, and twenty other men whom Eric's father had called to arms. Most of the men were well-trained soldiers while a number of them were knights. They were all loyal and able warriors who owed a service to Lord Braden for one reason or another.

We weren't a large party by any means, but we were sizeable enough to accomplish the coming task. We knew from Shelby that Cyrus had about twenty hired men, many of them whose fighting ability could be questioned. Cyrus could hire more men if needed, but he would have to know ahead of time that we were coming.

Our plan was to ride into Dereham and take the rapscallions by surprise. I would kill Cyrus and then his band of rogues would disassemble since they'd have no way of receiving further payment for their evil deeds. If for some reason it did come to an even battle, we figured the townsfolk would come to our aid.

To be sure that our arrival would be a surprise, we took a roundabout way to Dereham via an infrequently used road that was barely discernable from the woodland. Few people knew about it, but what was more important was that few people ever traveled on it, thus leaving a lesser chance of our party being seen by anyone. We projected that our course would take nearly four days to arrive, a day longer than the quickest route, but it would increase our chances of a successful trip.

Eric sent Peter and McCracken ahead to scout for any of Cyrus' men or anything else that might delay or jeopardize our party. If they saw something unusual they were to report back to us immediately. I again questioned Eric about McCracken's loyalty, but he assured me that he had no reason to distrust the man and he left it at that.

By the evening of our first day we found ourselves camped in a lush forest right outside the small town of Harlow. On Wednesday, we spent the night in a grassy meadow just beyond the town of Halstead.

Thursday morning I woke to a warm summer's rain. I opened my mouth and let the cool drops moisten my dry sticky tongue. It reminded me of the shower that had woken me so long ago, at least it seemed long ago. Actually, it had been but eight months since that cold wet morning when I laid in the forest barely alive.

Suddenly frightened, I rose upon my elbows and gazed around to be sure I hadn't dreamed all that had happened to me since that time. I felt comforted when I saw Donovan and heard him snoring loudly. My friend Eric was beside me and some of the soldiers were rising. I was safe and everything I had done since that awful day hadn't been just my imagination.

"Wake up Eric!" I yelled, slapping him on the back.

"What? Huh?" he mumbled with tired eyes blinking.

"The clouds are breaking and the sun shall soon be rising. Wake up!"

Eric rubbed his eyes, yawned, and then stood. As he folded his blanket, he said in a weary voice, "Rise men, we must be on our way!" Then he ambled over to his horse, put away his blanket, and untied the beast to let it graze.

I did the same and then I took some bread out of my pack. Before I ate, I made three signs of the cross in honor of the trinity and said a prayer.

"Good morning my lad." Donovan greeted me with a grin on his face. "Care for some ale? Ha! Just playing with you lad!" He tipped a jug up to his lips and drank. Ale spilled down his face and onto his tunic. "Ah, that's just what I need in the morning!"

"Where did you get that?" I asked.

"Tis my own secret!" answered Donovan with a brimming grin on his fleshy cheeks. "But if you must know, Lord Braden was kind enough to help out a thirsty soul."

"You're a tramp and a beggar!" I barked, shaking my head in scorn.

"That I am!" he exclaimed as he lifted the jug to his lips for another sip. "That I am!"

A quarter of an hour later all the men had eaten and packed their belongings. Soon we were on our horses and riding toward Dereham.

The rain had stopped and the sun began to stretch its lengthy fingers down onto the green countryside through the breaking clouds. The air was sweet and moist, as always, after an early morning summer shower.

While riding, the men were quiet. I believe they were enjoying, as I was, the beauty of the scenery around us. We crossed a glistening meadow of yellow grasses and wild flowers and came upon a common red fox. The wonderful animal stood silently sniffing the air with his snout bobbing up and down in a rhythmic motion, probably scenting his quarry or us. When we came too close, he darted off into the high grass.

Soon, our path led us into a lush green forest where the trees, wet and draped in moss, sparkled brilliantly in the sunlight. Flying nervously over our heads, a sparrow sung boisterously of our presence to the other beasts in the forest.

We crossed a babbling brook and enjoyed the sight of two deer, a mother and fawn, drinking from the cool churning water. They brought back the memory of the fawn I had seen months before in the grove of trees when I was so close to death. I still wondered why the animal had not been afraid of me.

As we came closer, our party stopped about fifteen yards away. The two animals still hadn't seen or smelled us yet and the flowing creek was covering up our sound. For a moment, I watched the two lovely beasts with wonder. Then, hearing a noise, I looked to my left and became horrified when next to me I saw Edward, a young knight in our party, drawing an arrow upon his bow.

"No!" I screamed, reaching forward and grabbing the reins of his horse.

Just then, Edward let go of his arrow and I watched it fly. It seemed like forever that the deadly instrument drifted though the air heading for its target.

The deer and fawn had heard me scream and they were now staring at us motionless as the arrow flew. Gazing into their dark brown eyes, it seemed to me that they were asking the question, "Why?"

Suddenly, the arrow thudded into a nearby tree and the two beasts turned their heads and peered at it. Then they glanced back at us for a moment before scrambling off over the brambles and fallen branches into the thick woods.

"Why did you do that?" asked Edward in a furious tone.

I wanted to answer him with my sword, but luckily I returned to my senses. What man wouldn't want fresh meat right now? I thought. After consuming stale bread and salted pork for the last two days, fresh venison would surely please the palate. Instead of being angry, I apologized and quickly began thinking up a reason for my behavior. "I'm greatly sorry Edward."

"Well, you right well should be!" he exclaimed with a gesticulating motion of his arms and trunk.

"We've not the time to clean and skin a deer," I said. "And besides, we've no idea of how close to us the king's foresters might be."

"The king's foresters? Bah! I've no fear of them. I'm a knight. I have the right to hunt deer or whatever else I like."

I glanced at Eric and he smiled while shrugging his shoulders in quandary.

"Yes Edward," I agreed, "you may have the right to hunt in the woods near your own village, but try convincing the Lord or Baron who's woods we're in right now that you have the right to hunt here."

"Well," he stammered, followed by stuttering and a few mumbled words.

Obviously, Edward understood the meaning of what I had said. I was thankful I had come up with such a good excuse for my bizarre actions so quickly, though I wasn't really sure why I did what I did. For some strange reason I just didn't want those two beasts harmed.

"Okay, let's get going before I have to use my broadsword on somebody," broke in Eric teasingly. A minute later we were on our way and I was glad that the whole situation was behind us.

As we went along, I began thinking about what Eric had just said and my eyes kept glancing at the enormous scabbard on his saddle. It contained his broadsword that was five feet in length and probably weighed more than six pounds. Few men had the skill and strength to use such a weapon with effectiveness. It requires two hands, so that when used in battle, the knight has to drop his shield and steer his horse with his knees. As a child, I had heard stories of soldiers dressed in armor being cut from shoulder to waist by masters of the broadsword. I could only hope that Eric had half that ability if we encountered Cyrus' men in combat.

Soon, our party entered another meadow and we saw two riders approaching. They turned out to be Peter the blacksmith and Ralph McCracken returning from their scouting duty.

"Greetings men. Seen anything out of the ordinary?" Eric asked as he brought his steed to a halt.

"Nothing except a few sparse peasants tending their fields," answered McCracken with a smile on his face.

"You're in a good mood today," I said, searching him with my eyes for a reason.

"And why not? Tis a beautiful day," he replied, lifting up his hands as if to display the day to me. Then he tugged on his scraggly beard, grinned with his rotten teeth showing, and winked at me.

This was the first time McCracken had been so friendly with me since I'd met him. Was he being sincere or was he trying to make the others laugh at my expense? I wasn't sure, but no one was laughing, so I took his gestures as a sign of friendliness. Maybe he had forgiven me for making him look like such a fool on the first night we'd met. If he had, he was a better man than I.

"Yes," I agreed, "it is a beautiful day. So you've seen nothing strange? No one asking questions? No travelers?"

Peter spoke up this time. "Oh we've seen travelers, after all it's summer, but nothing to suggest that they're Cyrus' men."

"Okay," said Eric. "You men have done a fine job so far. Now go on out ahead of us again and do the same. When all of this is over and done with, you will be well rewarded."

"Aye," I agreed, "not just from Eric and his father, but from me too."

Peter and McCracken nodded and then they galloped off with clumps of dirt flying from their beast's hoofs.

"Arrgh! You filthy dogs!" Donovan suddenly shouted in anger.

I turned to him to see what was wrong. He was wiping away a cluster of mud and grass from his left eye while muttering profanities underneath his breath. I began laughing and Donovan scowled at me.

"What's so amusing?" he asked, throwing the clump of mud in my direction.

"Come now Donovan, you know it's funny," I said.

"I, for one, don't think it's funny," he said as he reached for his jug of ale and took a long draw. Then his eyes swept over our troupe of men and he frowned sourly. "If I wasn't needed so much around here I'd be gone in a minute, and where would the lot of you be?"

It took all the self-control that the others and I had to hold back our laughter. None of us wanted to hurt Donovan's feelings by making him feel unimportant, though we all knew he would be useless in battle. He was good fun to have around and everyone enjoyed his company, so we kept our laughter to ourselves.

"George," Eric spoke up, "how far from Dereham are we now?"

"Well," replied Eric's stocky bald attendant, "if we ride till sundown tonight we should be near Swaffham. From there, we could make Dereham by early afternoon tomorrow."

"Good, then we'll be there two days before the wedding. Let's get moving."

Four hours later it was sundown and we found a place to camp near the town of Swaffham as George had predicted. It was a peaceful wooded area with a flowing creek and waterfall nearby.

As I lay awake that night, gazing at the stars and listening to the flowing creek, I wondered what the following day would bring to me. Would our party of men enter Dereham with no resistance? Would we surprise Cyrus' men or would they be waiting for us? Would I be able to defeat Cyrus one on one?

These questions flowed through my mind like the water that flowed between the rocks and pebbles in the nearby creek. I realized or finally admitted to myself that my greatest fear was of Cyrus. Though I was sure I was now a better swordsman than he, he had beaten me once, and that was enough to send a shiver up my backside. I could still see, just as clear as ever, his blade sticking out of my chest and him smiling sickly. I shook my head to drive away the terrible picture.

Sleep did not come quickly to me that night. It seemed that I stared at the stars in the clear sky above me for hours. Eventually though, my eyes grew weary and my mind began to drift. As I dozed off, my last thoughts were of Meranda. Would I see her tomorrow?

When daybreak came it brought with it a warm wind from the south. As our party rose, ate, and prepared for travel, I hurried quickly to the waterfall. I threw off my tunic, shirt and breeches, pulled off my stockings and boots, and dove into the pool beneath the falls.

I had no soap so I scrubbed myself with sand and pebbles from the bottom of the pool. The notion that I might possibly see Meranda that day was still in my head. If we did meet, I wanted to look my best.

I stood below the falls and rinsed off under the chilly water and gazed out at the forest around me. The leaf trees and underbrush were bright and colorful and the evergreens looked strong and stout. My ears were teased by the singing of birds and the splashing of water that produced a melody more wonderful than even the king's minstrels could create. I felt young and alive and capable of anything.

Smiling, I shook myself off and replaced my clothing. Then, with a light step, I made my way back to camp. When I returned I greeted Eric who was up and nearly ready to go. He was in a good mood too, as was everyone it appeared. Donovan was joking with the men as he drank his morning ale and they were all laughing at his silliness. It made me glad the portly peddler had come along.

When the laughter died down, we mounted our horses and continued on our way. It was Friday morning and by that afternoon we would be in Dereham, two days before the wedding. That would give us ample time to accomplish our goal even if we encountered trouble.

As we traveled, we passed a lake dotted with a few small fishing boats and we greeted some peasants as they worked the fields adjacent to the highway. Then we came to a fork in the road where a narrow path led away from the main one.

"This is where we cut off to Dereham," said Samuel, who was one of Lord Braden's knights. "I've been this way before."

I eyed Eric and asked, "What about Peter and McCracken, will they have gone this way?"

"Yes, Samuel drew up a map with complete directions before we left, and though he may not look it, McCracken is an expert map reader."

I glanced around at Eric's men for confirmation of McCracken's map reading skills and all of them nodded their heads in agreement. "Okay then," I said, "let's go."

We followed the meager path that was only wide enough for one horse to travel at a time. It led us down into a deep valley with steep hills on either side. The landscape was beautiful, scattered with wild flowers and conifers. A shallow stream flowed through the middle of the valley and paralleled our path.

"Look, there's smoke ahead of us!" exclaimed George.

I peered into the distance and shaded my eyes with my right hand to see better. Far off, in the light of the bright blue sky, I saw a long tall wisp of smoke.

"Looks like a camp fire," said one of the soldiers.

"Could be," said another.

We continued on and a half hour later we neared the origin of the smoke. We saw what appeared to be someone sleeping next to a smoldering fire and as we came closer we realized it was Peter.

Most likely thinking what I was thinking, which was that Peter wouldn't normally be sleeping that late in the morning, Eric leaped off of his horse and dashed up to him. "Peter! Wake up!" When Peter gave no answer, Eric began shaking him by the shoulders. When he still gave no reply, Eric pulled off the wool blanket covering him and threw it to the side. Suddenly, we all knew why Peter gave no response. On his tunic, in the center of his chest, was a large bright red stain.

"He's been stabbed!" screamed Eric.

"Ralph McCracken," I muttered underneath my breath.

"We shall see," replied Eric, glaring at me with a gaze of fury, "but remember Winston, there are thieves and cutthroats about. Just because you dislike the man doesn't mean I'm going to accuse him of murdering his friend without hearing what he has to say. That is, if he's not laying dead somewhere too!"

"I'm sorry," I quickly said. "I didn't know you would hear me and I shouldn't accuse a man so quickly. Especially one who's risked his life to save yours as you've told me he has done."

"I accept your apology Winston, but you are right in one sense."

"And what is that?"

"We must consider all possibilities, even treachery."

CHAPTER ELEVEN

"What's happened here?" bellowed a voice from behind us.

We all turned to see who had spoken. It was Ralph McCracken mounted on his horse and he was gazing at us as we stood over the body of Peter. No one in our party had heard him arrive, for all of us had been too caught up in the present situation.

Ralph jumped off of his horse, dashed to Peter's corpse, and knelt down beside it. "Peter!" he exclaimed. "Peter my friend! What have they done to you?" Then McCracken looked up and glared at us with dark searching eyes. He rose and pulled out his sword. "Which one of you did this? I shall kill you like a dog! Speak up!"

"Ralph!" Eric shouted. "It wasn't us! We found him like this! We thought you might know who did this?"

McCracken gazed at Eric for a moment and then his eyes fell to the ground. "I'm sorry sir, my rage overtook me for a moment."

"I understand," answered Eric, "we feel the same way."

While Eric and Ralph spoke, I was scrutinizing McCracken's reaction to his so-called friend's murder. I was skeptical that his grief was sincere and it appeared to me that his show of emotion had been rehearsed. If Ralph had nothing to cover up, why did he put on such a display? Did he really care for Peter that much? I doubted it.

"Why was Peter left alone?" Eric asked McCracken.

"You don't think I had a hand in this, do you?"

"No, of course not, but I'd like to know how this came to be."

"When we woke this morning, Peter was feeling ill and he wanted to sleep some more, so I told him he should. I said I'd scout around a bit and return later. That's what I did and when I came back you were here. A highwayman must have come and murdered him while he slept. Where's Peter's horse?"

"I've not seen it," replied Eric, peering around in all directions.

"I don't see his weapon either," said George.

"Ralph, you may be right," Eric said. "It appears that some scoundrel in need of a horse and weapon might have killed Peter while he slept."

"Wait a minute!" I protested. "Ralph could have just as easily frightened Peter's horse away and hidden his weapon to make it look like a robbery."

McCracken glared at me and his face turned red with what I presumed was rage, but he did not speak.

Eric eyed me with an air of frustration and annoyance, but then he turned to Ralph and asked, "How do you respond to that?"

"What would I accomplish by doing such a thing?" replied the scraggly bearded man. "What would I gain?"

Eric glanced back at me and I shrugged my shoulders, for I couldn't answer those questions. I was sure that McCracken had murdered Peter, but without a motive, I could press it no further.

"Well then," said Ralph, picking up a handful of dirt and tossing it back on the ground, "I guess that settles it. Peter—my poor friend—must have been murdered by a vile cutthroat while he slept. We'll have to inform the county steward as soon as possible. Now let's give Peter a proper burial."

"That we should!" clamored Edward who was followed in agreement by the rest of the men in our party.

A few minutes later, Eric's soldiers began digging a grave in the hard rocky earth alongside the stream that flowed through the center of the valley. Ralph went to fetch some branches in the underbrush to make a cross for the grave marker.

During this time, I kept thinking about what Ralph had said in regards to Peter being killed in his sleep. If that were the case, I determined, then the blanket we had found covering Peter's body should have a hole in it and be stained with blood where the blade had entered.

Not wanting to bring attention to myself, I slowly ambled over to the spot where we had found Peter's corpse. The blanket still lay in the grass nearby. While no one was watching, I spread the cloth out upon the ground and carefully inspected it. There was not a hole anywhere to be found and most certainly there was no hole in any area that would coincide with the location of Peter's mortal wound. Also, there were no bloodstains upon the blanket. The cloth must have been placed over Peter after his blood was dry and he was already dead.

Why would a highwayman stick around until his victim's blood had dried and then cover him with a blanket? He wouldn't I reasoned. Peter's killer must have been McCracken. McCracken may have even murdered the blacksmith the night before and then decided to cover him with the blanket at a later time.

But still the question "Why?" rang in my head. Why would he kill his comrade? What was his motive? I had no clue.

As Ralph finished the eulogy and the small ceremony for Peter was ending, I decided to tell Eric of my suspicions. I was motioning him to come over to me when something caught my eye far up on a hillside. It appeared as though an object had moved from behind an outcropping of rocks. I stared for a moment with searching eyes, but there was no further motion. Having an uneasy feeling that we were being watched, I gazed up toward the other side of the valley. Again, I noticed a quick movement that ceased abruptly.

An impending feeling of dread overcame me and suddenly I knew Ralph's motive. I pulled out my sword and bolted toward McCracken. "How much did he pay you?" I shouted.

Eric and his company of men turned toward me with a strange questioning glare as if I'd gone mad.

"Winston, what's got into you?" yelled Eric.

"It's a trap!" I cried. "Look around on the hillsides! We're surrounded!" Before I knew it, I was in front of McCracken and everyone else had backed away. He had his sword out and an expression of pure hatred encompassed his face.

"How much did Cyrus pay you?" I screamed again.

"I've no idea what you're talking about. But if it's a fight you want, then come on! I'm sober this time and I won't be made a fool of again!"

I was sick of his tongue and the lies that spewed from it, but I surprised even myself with my next action. McCracken swung his blade at me and I dodged it. Then I spun my body around and with one quick slice, his arm fell to the ground with sword in hand. As blood squirted from his stump, his eyes bulged in terror and I jabbed my blade into his chest. His scraggly bearded face turned pale with disbelief, but I felt no pity for him.

As the two of us stood there for a moment intertwined by a blade of steel, I gazed up at the hills. At least fifty horsemen on each side of the valley were racing down upon us. "See what he's done!" I cried, gesturing toward the hillsides.

McCracken fell to his knees and I pulled out my sword. Blood trickled from the corners of his mouth and a groan heaved from his chest as he expelled his last breath. Then he fell face first upon Peter's grave.

"Mount your horses men!" Eric commanded. "We shall retreat!"

Quickly I wiped off the blood from my blade onto McCracken's tunic. I climbed on my horse and kicked my spurs into the beast. Within seconds, the wind was blowing my hair back and the trees and bushes were rushing by. Finding myself in the middle of our retreating party, I glanced back to see where Eric was. He was in the rear letting all his men proceed before him. I slowed my horse and pulled off to the side of the path to wait for him. The riders flew by me in a blur of dust and as Eric passed, I entered the trail after him.

"You fool!" he exclaimed, though I could barely hear him over the rumbling of the horse's hoofs. "It's you they want, you should be in front!"

Paying no attention to him, I yelled, "What's your plan!"

"We must get out of this valley and reach a place where we can't be attacked on both flanks!"

I looked behind me as our horses took us swiftly up the path that we had originally come. Our enemy had reached the bottom where Peter and Ralph's campsite had been. They were regrouping and starting up the trail behind us.

"We've already accomplished our first goal!" I shouted. "They can't attack from two sides now!"

"Yes!" yelled Eric, "but still we must face them sooner or later!"

I peered behind me again and estimated Cyrus' men to be only a hundred yards away. I could see them clearly, but I didn't see the fat man himself. Coward, I thought.

"I'm sorry about McCracken—I was wrong about him!" exclaimed Eric.

I nodded, accepting his apology, but said nothing. We both knew Ralph had received what he deserved and that no further discussion was necessary.

Nearing the top of the valley, I saw an outcropping of rocks that I hadn't noticed earlier when coming down the trail. Behind the rocks was a grotto that went back into the hillside. "Eric!" I pointed to the ridge. "Do you see it?"

"Yes!" he replied, glancing back at our pursuers. "They're gaining on us, we've nothing else to do!"

Eric whistled at his men and when they looked back he pointed up toward the rocks. They nodded their heads in acknowledgment and steered their horses off of the main path and to the left leading them up the hillside.

As I turned my beast in the same direction, I noticed that one of our men continued up the established trail and disappeared over the crest of the hill. It was Donovan. The lousy tramp—he thinks only of himself! He has no honor—he's but a coward. Of course, I reasoned, what else should I expect from a man like him?

"They're right on our tail!" yelled Samuel, one of Eric's soldiers.

Immediately forgetting about Donovan, I gazed behind me and saw that Samuel was correct. I spurred my beast onward trying to escape the thunderous roar of hoofs pursuing us and drove quickly up the steep broken hillside.

Our party was nearly to the rocky outcropping when George's horse stumbled on some loose gravel. The animal fell backwards, landing on its rider's right leg. George cried out from the pain and then both he and his beast rolled and bounced down the rugged slope. The two of them came to a stop just yards away from our advancing enemies.

Instantly without thinking, I prodded my horse in the direction of George and raced toward him.

"No!" cried Eric, galloping after me.

I approached George and his eyes were open wide in terror. He was in a fury of panic, glancing back at his attackers while grappling at the coarse rocks before him. Sweat glistened from his bald crown as he pulled himself and his crushed leg up the hillside.

Suddenly I saw the glimmer of a blade and I knew my attempt at rescue was futile. A moment later, George's severed head was rolling down the rugged slope. His body still clung to the rocky incline as crimson furiously pulsated from its neck.

Engulfed with horror from the scene being played out before me, I forgot to keep an eye on my foes. When I realized my mistake, I looked up and found myself in the path of a knight. Fully fitted in armor, he was bearing down upon me with his sword raised high. Fear gripped me as my arm started in motion to lift my shield up for defense. It was too late though; the knight's sword was nearly upon me.

I waited for the pain to come when, unexpectedly and out of nowhere, I saw the shimmering of a broadsword heading in the direction of my foe. So quickly did it flash by my eyes that I hadn't the time to tell who was employing the weapon or whether it had hit my enemy or not. An instant later, I had to presume that the massive blade had missed my attacker, for he was still mounted on his horse and his sword continued to fall down upon me. Strangely though, as my foe lowered his blade, the weapon fell astray and missed me altogether. I realized then that the broadsword had actually struck my enemy, for the top half of his body tumbled to the rocky earth along with his weapon. The knight, armor and all, had been cut in two pieces at the waist. I watched in astonishment as the warrior's horse galloped up the hillside with only a pair of legs and hips mounted in the saddle.

Then quickly, I glanced around to orient myself and to see who had such skill with the broadsword. As I should have suspected, my eyes fell upon Eric. He was hacking away at our enemies, like a reaper harvesting wheat with a scythe, as they came up the rugged slope. I drove my horse in his direction, cutting and slashing my way through the men attacking me. "Eric! Head for the grotto!" I shouted.

"Yes! That was my idea you fool!"

A blade struck my shield and I swung my sword to knock it away. As I did, I gazed into the frightened eyes of my would-be killer. With a swift flip of my wrist, my blade sliced the man a wider mouth. "Let's go!" I called.

"Wait!" replied Eric as he swung his broadsword into the right front leg of a foe's horse. The beast fell and toppled its rider. "Okay, now!" he roared.

Turning, I kicked my spurs into the flanks of my horse and rushed up the mountainside. Our enemy stumbled over their dead and wounded which slowed them in their pursuit. When we reached the rocky knoll our animals leaped over the last few stones in our path and brought us into the grotto.

Eric's men had already dismounted and they were ready with lances, swords, and stones in an attempt to keep our attackers at bay. I jumped off of my beast and handed the reins to Edward. He took the horse back into the large cavern with the others.

Our enemy came forward and though there were many of them, they seemed to be clumsy and disorganized on the steep rocky hillside. Only a few appeared to be trained knights while the rest were merely hired cutthroats at best. As they approached us, we thrust lances and threw heavy stones upon them. Unprepared for the damage this caused, they quickly retreated after suffering a number of casualties.

"You can't stay up there forever!" yelled one of our enemies far below us. "We only want Winston! If you give him up, none of you will be harmed!"

Eric laughed and bellowed, "If you want him so badly, come and get him!" Then he turned to me and slapped my shoulder with the back of his hand. "Let's go inside Winston."

We entered the grotto, which we were very lucky to have found, for it made a natural fortress. It had an opening about eight yards wide by roughly three yards high and it was much larger on the inside than I had expected. The cavern must have been found and used by earlier peoples at one time, for the earthen floor had been mostly cleared of the smaller rocks and rubble. However, there were still numerous heavy rocks and boulders scattered throughout the enclosure. At the entrance to the cave, there were large piles of stones that would serve us well, and had probably served others, as artillery against any assaults. Additionally, the grotto extended into the hillside at least sixty feet where a clear pool was formed by water seeping from the rocky wall. Thus, we had ample room and plenty of fresh water for our men and our beasts. It would have been difficult for even a great army to attack and defeat us in such a strategic location.

For the rest of that day, Eric's men kept a watch out for our enemy at the entrance while Eric and I discussed our plans. We presented various strategies to each other on how we could best escape the grotto, but all of our ideas led us to one conclusion; that without outside help, escape would be near suicide for our small party of men. This disappointed me greatly, for I so wanted to get to Dereham and save Meranda from Cyrus' vileness.

We spent that night in the grotto under a full moon. Eric had two of his soldiers, Samuel and Randolph, keep watch from dusk to dawn. Fortunately, our enemies showed no signs of themselves.

We woke to a sunny day with a light warm breeze blowing through the valley, but a feeling of uncertainty clouded the air. We all wanted to move on, especially me, since it was Saturday and the next day was Meranda's wedding. A good reasonable plan was still needed, but none was available. I was desperate to leave the grotto and my frustration began to wear on me.

"Couldn't we make a run for it?" I asked Eric, as he took a chunk of dried pork out of his knapsack for breakfast.

"That we could," he replied, tearing at the meat with his teeth and chewing on it fiercely. "But if we ride out through the middle of them, many of us will be slaughtered like pigs. And these men aren't mine to toss away. They owe only a service to my father, not their lives."

"But what of Meranda—what will happen to her?"

Eric stood silent for a moment, chewing his food and gazing at the ground. He didn't answer me.

"We have to be in Dereham by tomorrow!" I shouted.

"I'm sorry Winston, but it may not be possible. You know my father will be waiting for word from us. When it doesn't arrive, he'll come to our aid with more men than we can count, but it probably won't be for a few days."

"That's great!" I yelled in anger. "By then Meranda will have been defiled by that serpent Cyrus! I don't know why I ever came to you for help in the first place!" I stormed off to the other end of the grotto and sat down in the darkness by myself.

I was mad. I didn't want Meranda to marry Cyrus and selfishly I didn't care how many men had to die to stop the wedding. I'll sneak off in the night by myself, I reasoned. I'm not scared to leave this ledge of safety. I'll kill the fat man myself, along with anyone else who gets in my way for that matter.

As I wallowed in my anger and self-pity, I eventually came to realize that Eric was right. There were too many men surrounding us and it would have been suicide for our party to try and fight them all. I also knew in my heart that if I attempted to go alone, the chances of getting to Cyrus without being killed by his men first were slim at best. We would have to wait it out.

"Move back! Get under the cliff!" exclaimed one of our men suddenly.

I looked out toward the entrance of the cavern and saw Randolph. He was motioning to everyone who was resting out on the rocky knoll to get inside.

"They're above us!" he screamed.

I moved closer to the entrance to see what was occurring. There were five men outside and they cried out in pain as stones began pelting them from above. Leaping over the rugged terrain, they covered their heads with their arms and scrambled to safety as fast as they possibly could. Then a loud crack rang out and Samuel fell to the ground face first. A huge stone which wasn't there a moment before laid beside him. Edward and Randolph quickly rushed to his side, picked him up, and brought him into the grotto.

I raced over to them as they set Samuel down. Blood oozed from a cavity in the back of his head and a grayish substance was visible where part of his skull was missing. His body began to shake violently and Edward and Randolph tried to hold him still. Saliva foamed from his mouth and his eyes rolled back and forth in their sockets.

Just then, the last two men, Douglas and Phillip, came charging inside.

"Are you two okay?" asked Eric.

"Fine," replied Douglas breathing heavily, "but I think Phillip here has broken his arm."

We all glanced at Phillip who was holding his left elbow. "I'll be alright," he said as the last few stones hit the earth outside and then became silent.

After knowing that everyone else was safe, we focused our attention back on Samuel. Randolph and Edward were still holding him, trying to keep his body from constantly writhing.

"What are we going to do?" screamed Edward. "Look at him!"

"I see him!" yelled Eric.

"What's wrong with him?" asked Randolph.

"He's got a demon in him!" replied Edward.

I was trying not to look at Samuel, for his horrific display was making me sick, but I glanced at him again. His eyes, wild and glazed, were still rolling about in his head and his legs gesticulated uncontrollably. Blood began to ooze from his mouth as his jaw opened and closed in rhythmic fashion continuously biting his tongue.

"Somebody do something!" cried Edward.

"What—what can we do?" exclaimed Eric trembling as droplets of sweat glistened off of his pale face.

The other men in our party circled about to see what was happening. As they gazed upon Samuel, their faces turned pale too.

"What are you staring at? Get away!" barked Eric. Then he pointed out toward the cavern opening with his right hand. "Andrew! Charles! Go to the ledge and keep an eye on our enemy! They may attempt an attack now! And keep an eye out above you!"

The two men did as they were told while the rest of us stood by Samuel. The sight of him afflicted us all, but none of us had any idea what to do. We'd never seen such a ghastly sight.

Then abruptly, Samuel let out a loud dreadful hissing sigh and his writhing body ceased to move. Edward and Randolph released his arms and his body settled to the earth.

Eric turned away from the sight. "How's it look out there?" he asked Andrew and Charles.

"Nothing out here and no movement above us," replied Charles.

I stumbled out to the rocky knoll followed by most of the men. None of us wanted to gaze upon Samuel's lifeless corpse. I saw our enemy and their smoking campfires below us in the valley. Then I spotted two riders off to my left on the hillside and I watched them as they came toward us. They stopped about fifty yards away.

"Now will you give up Winston Tabor?" called out one of the riders.

Eric stepped up next to me and put his hand on my shoulder. "Never!" he howled.

"Then we shall wait!" exclaimed the horsemen, raising his fist high into the air.

For a moment I stood there watching, then suddenly I realized what the man was doing. "Inside everyone! Get back inside!" I shouted as I turned myself around and raced back into the grotto.

While scurrying over the rocks and gravel, I heard a tremendous roar. As I had suspected, it was another landslide of rocks. Once I was safely inside I turned around and peered into the dust and debris to see if everyone else had made it.

"Well done Winston!" bellowed Eric, his face instantly appearing out of the dark haze of dust.

"Did everyone make it in this time?" I asked.

"Yes," replied Eric. "I should have known when that rider waved his fist in the air that he was signaling his men on the cliff to drop more stones. It's a good thing you saw it coming or we'd all be in the same condition as Samuel."

"I almost didn't notice it."

"Well you did and that's all that matters. I just wish there was some way we could get out of this mess by tomorrow so that we could make it to Dereham."

"I know you do Eric," I said, "and I want to apologize for shouting at you earlier. You're right about staying here until your father comes. There's no sense in trying to fight a hundred men with the few we have here."

"We should have brought more men—I should have brought more men," replied Eric. "Why was I such a fool?"

"It's not your fault. We didn't know Cyrus had so many hired rogues."

"He wouldn't have had so many if it weren't for Ralph McCracken. Cyrus probably knew we were coming before we'd even left my father's estate. How could I have trusted such a man as McCracken?"

"You did what you believed was right. He had never caused you any reason to distrust him, had he?"

"No. Never."

"Well then, your judgment was sound. You had no idea he would become a traitor just because he disliked me for making a fool out of him one night in a tavern."

Eric nodded in agreement. "I guess you're right Winston, but still I wish we could get out of this mess by tomorrow."

"So do I," I said, "so do I."

*   *   *

The day slowly wore on until dusk found me resting beside a rock in the twilight of the grotto. We'd heard nothing more from our enemy and there was little for us to do but sit tight and wait. Becoming weary, I closed my eyes and soon my thoughts were of Meranda. I saw her standing on the bank of the stream where we had first met, her long golden hair dancing in the breeze and her eyes of blue gazing into mine. She was speaking to me, but I couldn't hear what she was saying. Then, while reaching out to touch her, I fell into slumber.

CHAPTER TWELVE

A piercing scream and a resounding thud awoke me. It was still dark outside as I groggily stood and pulled my sword from its scabbard. I presumed our watchmen had been foolish and had fallen asleep leaving us susceptible to a surprise attack. At any moment, I believed the enemy would be upon me. Instead, my ears again were filled with a deafening scream and a disquieting thud.

"They're falling from the cliff!" yelled one of Eric's soldiers.

"Who's falling from the cliff?" I heard another ask.

There was confusion in the grotto as everyone awoke. It was dark and men were bumping into each other and asking, "Who's there?"

"Don't draw your swords on one another!" I heard Eric bellow. "We're not under attack! Everyone, come to the entrance!"

Stumbling, I found my way remarkably quickly through the darkness to the entrance of the grotto. Once there, I gazed above the cavern opening where some sort of commotion was occurring. Men were shouting and the pattering of footsteps echoed from the rocky ledge. I strained my eyes to see better and suddenly the silhouette of a man appeared falling from the ridge above. In the moonlight I saw the individual twisting and turning to regain his balance as he plunged toward the earth. His wriggling was useless, for a moment later I heard again the now familiar and sickening thud as his body crashed upon the rugged slope.

After our party watched this event in amazement, I peered down into the valley and saw torches being lit. It appeared as though our enemy was arising from the commotion and knew nothing more than we did about the disturbance above us on the cliff.

"What's going on up there?" Edward asked, eyeing Eric for an answer.

"I don't know, but it appears as though our enemy's lookouts are falling from the cliff above us and I like it," replied Eric.

Edward smiled showing a number of decaying teeth.

"Men!" yelled Eric. "Get our horses, this may be our best chance to escape! Remember though, we don't know who or what is causing this! It could be friend or foe! Be careful!"

As Eric's men retrieved our horses, I heard what sounded like footsteps on the gravely slope to the left of the grotto. I readied my blade for an attack, not knowing who or what might appear. An instant later, at the corner of the rocky knoll, a man stepped out from behind a boulder. I moved toward him and squinted my eyes. Could it be? I wondered. In the dim light it was hard to tell, but the pudgy face before me resembled that of Donovan's.

"Ho ho ho, my lad! I'm here to save you!"

"Donovan, what are you doing here? Who is with you—there is somebody with you—isn't there?"

Donovan laughed again. "Of course there is! You think I'd come alone?"

"I didn't think you would return at all to tell you the truth," I replied grinning. "But for a moment I had a dreadful feeling you were foolish enough to come back by yourself!"

"Ha ha ha! Come on now," he cackled, gesticulating his hands, "we'd better be on our way."

Just then, another familiar face appeared from around the boulder. It was Lord Stanton. "William!" I exclaimed, reaching out my hand to shake his.

"Winston my boy, I didn't expect to see you so soon!" he roared, glancing down into the valley and then looking back at me with his deep dark eyes. "Seems you're in a bit of trouble."

"Yes, you see—"

"Don't bother explaining," he said, pointing toward Donovan, "this man has already told me of your plight. We must get along now if we want to prevent that young girl from becoming Cyrus' wife, now shan't we?"

"Yes," I agreed.

Lord Stanton smiled and winked.

Then I turned to Eric and said, "This is my friend, Lord Stanton."

William greeted Eric cordially and then asked, "How many men does the enemy have?"

"At least a hundred," answered Eric.

"And how many of you?"

"We're down to twenty-four including Donovan," I said.

"How many are with you?" Eric asked of William.

"Seventy," he replied, "so it seems we're fairly even. Now let's go before we lose what little surprise we still have!"

We grabbed our horses by the reins and guided them out of the grotto and up the rocky winding path to the top of the cliff. When we arrived, all of Lord Stanton's knights and soldiers were waiting for us. The knights Richard, Arthur, Stewart, Walter, David, Joseph, and John all greeted me with a handshake or a nod.

Glancing around, I saw what had happened to Cyrus' men who had been stationed up on the ridge. Those who had not been hurled to the rocky hillside below lay strewn on the grassy meadow around us, blood still seeping from their mortal wounds.

"Silence!" William suddenly called out.

Everyone became motionless for a moment and listened. A thundering of hoofs was heard in the distance and I peered toward the valley below. Torches now lit the rocky slopes on either side of the grotto and our enemy was getting closer with every second.

"Half of you men will go that way," commanded William, motioning to the right of the cliff. "The other half will follow me. We'll meet in the valley once we defeat them. Now go!"

Our gathering broke up into two separate parties. One group headed to the left and the other to the right of the grotto. Eric trotted off toward the right side with most of his men and I was going to join him when William spoke. "Winston, follow me."

I looked at him and he turned to Sir Richard and motioned for him to hand me something. Sir Richard held out a lance.

I took it from him and gazed at William with searching eyes. "I'm better with a sword," I said.

"Nonsense, you're quite capable with a lance," he replied. Then he dug his spurs deep into the flanks of his horse and galloped off down the trail. "Come my lad!"

I followed him down the curvaceous rocky trail and was surprised that my steed could manage the slope with me riding upon him. Below us I saw the glowing torches of our enemies and as we rounded a corner, I heard the sound of sword upon sword. It appeared that our front line was already beset in combat.

As the new day's sun was just beginning to deliver the light of dawn, I spurred my horse to hasten him on. Soon I could see the enemy. Approaching a foe, I lowered my rod and prepared for the impact. He desperately attempted to knock my lance away with his sword and protect himself with his shield, but he could not. Though he wore a helmet, his visor was up and I could see his eyes become wide and glossy as he watched the point of my rod puncture his thin armor plating. In an instant, my lance skewered his torso and exited out of his backside. He screamed in agony, but his cry was muffled by his helmet and the thunder of battle. Passing him, his body pivoted with me, so I pulled on my lance and it came out the front side of him. Crimson gurgled from the unfortunate rider's mouth and his quivering corpse fell to the earth. I turned away from him and spurred my horse on, wanting to fight some more.

Immediately, I came upon a knight riding up the rugged terrain. He carried a lance and as we met, both our spears hit each other's shields at the same time. A resounding crack rang out and the force of the blow jolted me to the ground with a painful thud.

I stood up quickly and at the same time pulled my sword from its scabbard and prepared for another assault. I looked at my enemy's horse, but my foe was not mounted upon it. I turned and saw him lying on the ground and he was slow in rising. I dashed over to him and found that he was in full harness, which explained his difficulty in getting up. Fortunately, I hadn't had time to don the armor that Lord Stanton had given me before leaving the grotto. Thus, I remained much more nimble and agile than my foe.

As he tried to stand I kicked him in the side and he fell over onto his back. I placed my sword up to his groin and asked, "Do you surrender?"

This left the man two choices. If he was too proud and refused surrendering, then I would humanely kill him by thrusting my blade between the two plates of armor at his groin and slice open an artery. If he surrendered, then he would have to make me his equal by knighting me, for a knight can only surrender to the same.

"Have you been given the accolade?" he asked.

"No, I'm an armiger and have received my sword in ceremony, but I've not been knighted."

"You have the ability of a knight, therefore I have no shame in surrendering to you."

I smiled, knowing that I would now be knighted. Additionally, though I didn't care about it at that moment, I would also be paid a ransom from his family or overlord for his safe return. If they didn't pay, I would eventually free him, but I would sell his destrier and armor for a handsome sum.

I reached down and helped my foe to his feet. When he had fully risen, I picked up his sword and handed it to him. "You'll need this," I said, kneeling for the accolade.

The knight gently tapped both of my shoulders with the tip of his sword. "In the name of God and as Heaven as my witness, I dub thee knight," he pronounced.

A cheer rang out and I glanced behind me to see from where it had come. A few of Lord Stanton's men, who had completed their fighting for the moment, were watching me. They yelled and clapped their hands.

My enemy handed me his blade and I gave him over to William's men. "Keep him safe," I said, "for he is a gallant knight."

Then, just as I was beginning to wonder what had happened to my horse, Sir David rode up with the beast and handed me the reins. After thanking him, I mounted the animal and galloped toward the battleground that had moved further down into the valley. A few minutes later, after traveling a path that was strewn with dead and wounded men, I arrived at the valley floor. There I came upon Lord Stanton and Eric riding side by side.

"Well my boy," said William with a grin, "it looks like we've got Cyrus' men on the run."

"Thanks to you," I replied.

"It wasn't just me," said William.

"I know, but without you and your men we'd still be stuck in that grotto."

"Yes, that's true," agreed Eric.

"Well, you should also be grateful to Donovan for coming to me and asking for help," replied William.

"Yes, I am grateful. I was sure he had run away and would never come back."

"I think what you did in Hertford earned you a friend for life," said William.

"I imagine so," I replied. Then I asked, "Where is Donovan now?"

"I haven't seen him," answered William.

"I'm sure the fool will turn up sooner or later," replied Eric.

"We better get moving if we're going to catch up with the rest of my men," said William.

Eric and I agreed, so we prodded our horses and a moment later we were galloping in the direction of Dereham.

When we caught up to the main core of William and Eric's men, Cyrus' few remaining knights and mercenaries were retreating briskly. Their skill in battle had been lacking compared to those of the knights and soldiers in our party. Still, we continued to chase them along the valley floor and up into the piney hillsides as the morning sun was rising.

"We've got those cowards on the run now, eh?"

I turned to see who had spoken and it was Donovan. His fleshy jowls bounced with each gallop of his horse and the wind had colored his cheeks a deeper red than usual.

"Yes, we sure do," I said, "and it's due to your bravery."

"Ah, it was nothing. Though I told you I'd be of service to you. I told you I'd pay you back for helping me out."

"You certainly did. You're a good man, Donovan."

He smiled brightly, appearing genuinely happy with himself. Something, I perceived, he hadn't felt in a good long time.

Our party began to slow its pace as we realized that none of Cyrus' men were stopping to fight anymore. Soon, we watched the last of their disorganized band of ruffians gallop over the top of the valley's edge and disappear into the horizon. My spirits were high and I was ready to ride into Dereham to avenge my father and stop the wedding of Cyrus and Meranda.

William brought his horse to a trot and everyone else followed suit. The knights and soldiers of our party cheered and raised their arms in victory. A moment later, Sir John rode up to us, having just returned from the valley floor.

"What are our casualties?" Lord Stanton asked him.

"We lost three men sir."

"How many wounded?"

"About twenty or so, most of them minor."

"Did we capture any knights?"

"Among the few knights who fought alongside those filthy rogues, we captured two. Another wouldn't be taken alive, so he was put to the knife."

"All right then, pick ten men and return to the manor with those who are severely wounded. Take the two captives along with you."

"Yes my lord," replied Sir John, "I might add sir, that it was Winston who took one of the knights single handedly."

"Well," said Lord Stanton smiling broadly and gazing at me with his dark intense eyes. "Congratulations Winston! Or should I say Sir Winston?"

"Thank you sir," I replied, feeling quite pleased with myself and happy that Lord Stanton was now aware of my accomplishment.

A few moments later, after Eric and Donovan congratulated me also, William cried, "Onward men!" and our party galloped up the final yards of the valley's slope. Once we ascended its crest, a broad sweeping meadow opened up before us. It was laden with grasses, colorful wild flowers, and a number of scattered oak trees. Covered in morning dew, the meadow sparkled brilliantly in the early day's light.

Enticed by its beauty, I let my eyes wander outward across its broad expanse and to the horizon. Far out in the distance, I saw what seemed to be a thin dark shadow stretching from left to right. Squinting hard, I quickly realized it was our enemy and they had regrouped. Did they want to receive another thrashing? I pondered.

We rode a short distance further and I noticed there was one knight mounted on his steed positioned about twenty yards in front of the line of our enemy. A shiver ran up my spine when I realized that the knight's armor was black.

"Only the vilest of men who crawl upon this earth would hire the Dark Knight," uttered Lord Stanton in abhorrence.

"Is that really him?" I asked.

"Only he who wears the black ribbon on his helmet and carries the black banner can be called the Dark Knight."

We continued onward toward our enemy. A moment later I could make out a ribbon fluttering from the horseman's helmet and a banner at the end of his lance waving in the breeze. Both pieces of cloth were black.

"How many men do you figure are behind the dark one?" asked Eric as he trotted up along side of us.

"It appears to be the same group and same number of men we chased out of the valley," I replied.

"Yes," said William, "but it's not them we need worry about. One of us must accept the challenge of the Dark Knight."

"I will kill him," I said.

"It's not so easy," replied William, "he has never lost and any man who faces him will probably die."

I took a deep breath realizing the truth in the words Lord Stanton had spoken. If any man should fight the Dark Knight, I knew it was I, but fear was rising up within me from the deepest recesses of my childhood. I had long believed the Dark Knight was but a myth. Now he was here, across this magnificent field, waiting for me.

Swallowing hard, I spoke. "It's for my family and my small fiefdom which brings us here today, therefore, it is I who must be willing to pay the ultimate price." I turned to Sir Walter who had come up alongside of me. "Please Sir, give me your lance." He handed it over to me with an understanding nod of his head. I spurred my horse and headed out into the meadow.

"No wait!" yelled the familiar voice of William, galloping toward me. "Let it be me!"

"No, I can't!" I replied, stopping my horse. William grabbed my arm and squeezed it hard. "Unhand me!" I shouted.

"Give me the chance Winston! I've fought him many times in my dreams! I've waited for this day for years!"

"But what if you're killed?"

"Then I join my wife and my son in death. Don't you see? I've nothing to lose. But you my lad—you have everything to lose. There's a girl who waits for you. Now give me the chance Winston!"

I gazed into William's dark eyes and a few curly strands of his long black hair fell around them.

"Please!" he begged, grabbing my arm tightly again.

"Alright!" I said, and as quickly as the word had left my lips, I felt ashamed.

"Thank you my son," William quietly uttered as he took his hand away from my arm. Then he galloped off across the field with his lance held high and his polished armor shimmering in the sunlight.

After approaching the enemy, Lord Stanton stopped fifty yards off and faced the Dark Knight. He lowered his visor and nodded to his opponent. The two men leveled their spears and commenced their attack. A moment later they were upon each other.

William's lance hit the center of his foe's shield and I was sure the force of it would impale or dismount the Dark Knight. I was wrong however, for the rider in black was able to swing his shield to the side and knock the tip of William's pole away from him. At the same time, the Dark Knight thrust his lance at Lord Stanton and it appeared to be a deadly strike. Luckily though, in the last instant, William was likewise able to block the jab away with his shield.

The two men circled back and around to prepare for another attack. They stopped for a moment, nodded at one another, and then proceeded to come together. Again, both men were on target, their rods hitting directly in the center of each other's shield. It looked as though both knights would be dismounted when suddenly a thundering snap fulminated from William's lance. The long pole splintered into fragments and Lord Stanton was thrown backward and out of his saddle by his opponent's spear.

William seemed to emerge unhurt except for the pain of being knocked to the ground. Thankfully, the point of the Dark Knight's rod had not found William's flesh and had done nothing but flung him from his horse.

As Lord Stanton attempted to stand in full harness, the evil knight abruptly turned around and prodded his beast into a gallop. "No!" I found myself yelling as I watched him come at William from behind.

Still trying to stand up entirely, Lord Stanton was unaware of his enemy's position and didn't see the impending cowardly attack. He was helpless and I gaped in horror as the Dark Knight raced from behind and rammed his spear through the center of William's back.

A surge of anger and a wave of grief rippled through my body and before I knew it, I was galloping over the meadow toward Lord Stanton. When I arrived, I leaped off of my horse and went to him. "William! William!" I cried, wrapping my arms around him and removing his helmet. William's men came riding over as I placed his head upon my lap.

"Winston," he whispered as blood ran from his lips, "you can beat him."

"No William!" I protested. "We're going to take you home!"

"I'm going home," he said, "but not to Hertford."

"No, you can't leave us! We haven't finished!"

"You must finish it Winston—it's time I join my wife and son."

Eric put his hand on my shoulder and nodded in agreement with Lord Stanton. I glanced around at the others and they were shaking their heads in assent too.

"Father, forgive me," whispered William. "Please receive me when I knock upon your door."

William's body went limp and I rested his head on the ground. In his eyes I saw the reflection of the clear blue sky and I knew God had answered his prayer.

As I kneeled there in the dewy meadow staring in disbelief at the lifeless body before me, I heard a deep booming cackle behind me. I cocked my head and there, over my shoulder upon his ebony horse, was the Dark Knight. A furious rage exploded within me causing my body to shake uncontrollably. I jumped on my horse with one quick leap and, without asking for it, Sir Richard shoved a lance in my hands.

The Dark Knight spurred his horse and galloped out into the meadow leaving a trail of laughter behind him. He came to a halt and turned his destrier around to face me. Then, as if to mock me, he raised his lance high into the air and showed off its blood stained pennon that fluttered in the breeze.

My heart pounded with hatred for the evil man and I started after him. When he saw this, he too incited his horse and raced toward me. By chance, the low morning sun was behind me and its long reaching fingers stretched directly into the eye slits of the Dark Knight's visor. I could tell he was having trouble seeing me. I lowered my lance and aimed for his abdomen just below his shield.

As the two of us came together, I noticed that my enemy's spear was entirely off its target, so I concentrated solely on driving my lance into his midsection. Just when I believed my pole was about to impale the foul warrior, he lowered his shield and remarkably prevented my weapon from causing any harm. My enemy's lance grazed my side but inflicted no wounds. As we passed each other, I again heard his dreadful laugh and a tinge of fear shuddered through my body.

The next thing I knew, I was heading toward the drawn-out row of Cyrus' cutthroats. While turning my horse around for another attack, they howled and jeered at me. What cowards, I thought. They would be running from us if it weren't for the Dark Knight.

A moment later, I began another charge across the vast grassy meadow and this time the sun was facing me. It blazed relentlessly into my eyes, nearly causing me to hit one of the few oak trees that grew sparsely throughout the field. After narrowly avoiding the tree, I began to make out a dark shape approaching me in the glare of sunlight. I thrust my lance blindly in its direction. My weapon hit empty space and I quickly realized that I had little control over the situation. Fear took me into its grasp and I braced myself for the blow that was sure to come. But to my delight, the blow never came. The Dark Knight's horse stepped into an unseen hole, causing it to stumble recklessly. My foe's lance missed me again. My companions, who had been watching in dismay, cheered in elation.

While a feeling of relief washed over me, my enemy's horse suddenly regained its balance and lashed out at me as I rode by. Snapping and biting, the well-trained beast drew blood from my shoulder. Ignoring the pain, I circled around to prepare for another attack.

My comrades cheered as I galloped passed, giving me more strength and courage to continue to fight. The sun was in my favor once more and my rage and fear were giving away to reason. I spurred my horse on and raced swiftly over the meadow.

Lowering my lance, I aimed for the center of my opponent's chest. I could tell that, even with his helmet and visor, my adversary was having trouble with the sun's rays again. It appeared he couldn't see the tip of my rod and he didn't know where to place his shield to protect himself. I, on the other hand, clearly saw his lance coming toward me and I was able to knock it away with my shield. Just as I did, I felt the blow of my spear striking the Dark Knight's armor and I watched with glee as his body twisted backward.

A joyous feeling overcame me and I almost cried out in jubilation, but my triumph lasted only a moment. When I gazed down at the end of my rod, it unfortunately was not piercing my enemy's torso. Instead, the metal spike had broken off, leaving a dull rounded tip. The Dark Knight rode past me unscathed.

Dismayed, I brought my destrier to a halt and found myself staring into the faces of a string of filthy rogues. They howled and cackled as they pointed at my dull spear. I wanted to rush them and kill as many as I could with my sword before they took my life, but I knew that would surely mean the end of all my hopes and dreams. I had only one chance and, though it was slight, it laid in the opposite direction. I reeled my horse around.

Forty yards away, in the bright glare of the sun, was perched the Dark Knight upon his steed. He reached up to his left shoulder plate with his right hand and pulled out the metal tip of my lance. He then tossed it carelessly behind him with a sinister laugh.

My mind was racing forward and I found myself trembling. If this were a tournament, I reasoned, my squire could give me a fresh lance, or if I was on the other side of the meadow Eric could toss me a new one. But I wasn't in a tournament and I was on the wrong side of the meadow. There were too many ifs. I had to act.

Suddenly an idea came to me, it was far fetched, but it was my only chance. I gazed out over the trampled meadow and eyed the nearest oak tree. It was just to my right, the same one I had nearly hit earlier. With a kick of my heels and a quick prayer, I galloped off heading in the direction of my opponent and the oak.

Approaching the Dark Knight, I heard his deep roaring laugh echo across the field. He must have presumed I was a fool to attack him with only a dull lance as a weapon. And I may well have been a fool, for if my plan were to work it would only be by the good grace of God.

The sun was in my eyes and my foe became a dark blur in the blazing light. Within seconds, the evil man was but twenty yards away. As I passed the oak tree, I stuck the end of my lance out to the right of me and into its branches. A resounding crack pierced the air as my rod shattered lengthwise leaving a long sharp splinter at the end. Blindly, I raised my shield to cover my body and at the same time I lifted up the broken rod and thrust it forward not knowing where it would strike.

At the same instant, I was pounded with a fierce blow from the Dark Knight's spear. It hit my shield forcing me backward and knocking me off of my steed. As I soared through the air, I caught a glimpse of my foe. He had let go of his lance and his hands moved upward toward his face. They were desperately grasping for something that jutted out from the left eye slit of his visor. A high shrilling cry rang out over the meadow as crimson gushed from the tragic figure's helmet.

I hit the ground with a crushing blow, knocking the breath from me. The Dark Knight tumbled over the grassy sod and came to rest on his back next to me. As I tried to regain my breath, I turned my head and recognized what had caused my enemy's devastation. It was the jagged tip from my broken lance. Blood flowed from his visor and his body shook violently. Then he was still.

Cheers filled the air around me as Eric's and William's men rode over to commend me. I stood, after regaining my breath, and greeted them.

Then I marched over to the fallen knight as crimson continued to ooze from his helmet. Glaring at the wide row of cutthroats and bandits, I pointed to the dead man. "This is what happens when you cross Winston Tabor!" My body trembled with anger. "Who shall be next?" A murmur was heard throughout the rapscallion's ranks, but not one man came forward. I took a step toward them. "I'm going to Dereham to avenge the death of my mother and father! Those who stand in my way shall die!" There was no reply from the line of dumbfounded rogues who stared at me from atop their horses. They appeared to be in shock at the sight of the Dark Knight lying bloodied in the meadow before them.

Just then, Sir Richard led my horse over to me and handed me the reins. "We're still with you," he said, "it would have been Lord Stanton's will."

I nodded and mounted my steed. Then I pulled my sword from its scabbard and raised it high above me. "Attack!" I shouted.

Side by side, our metal blades gleaming in the brilliant sun, we charged the row of ruffians with a guttural roar. The miscreants stood their ground for a moment, but after a number of them were cut down they quickly turned and galloped away.

We chased them for a few minutes to be sure that they wouldn't later regroup and attack, but soon it was obvious that the cowards had given up completely. We watched as the last of them rode off in aimless directions.

CHAPTER THIRTEEN

We drove our horses at a steady gallop and headed for Dereham, which was only an hour's ride away. I prayed to God that I still had time enough to stop the wedding between Cyrus and Meranda. I knew that even if I could defeat Cyrus and avenge my parents, I would still feel as though I had failed if I couldn't prevent Meranda from marrying such a foul man. My feelings were therefore mixed. Delight and anticipation arose within me knowing that soon I would see Meranda, but apprehension and fear of what I might find when I arrived also filled my mind. In addition, sadness continued to pervade my heart over the death of Lord Stanton.

Worst, however, of all the feelings that flowed through my soul was a deep dark awareness of true fear that kept creeping into my mind. I had been trying to push it away for a long time, but the closer I came to possibly seeing Cyrus again the more it grew. An apparition of the fat man withdrawing his sword from my chest flashed in front of my eyes. It seemed so real that I trembled and shook. I felt I might fall from my horse, but fortunately I did not. Horrified at my own cowardice, I realize that Donovan had truly been correct. I had been purposely delaying my encounter with Cyrus Everett. I could have asked for Lord Stanton's help long ago and maybe he would be alive now if I had. I really was afraid of the beast of a man Cyrus. I wasn't sure if I could face him, let alone fight him. What was I to do? I wondered. Then I stole a quick glance at the men's faces riding along side of me, so as to be sure they didn't notice my fearful irresolution. Their faces were determined, as if etched in stone; they were not frightened. This made me feel shameful, but also it emboldened me somewhat. I swallowed my fear as best I could and rode on.

Then, determining that the sooner I faced my fear the better it would be, I kicked my spurs into the flanks of my horse. I raced as swiftly as possible toward Dereham with my party of men following behind. The sun was now high and a soft warm wind blew from the south as our path merged with a road. We dashed past a collection of green fields and I recognized the land. It was the sweet fertile acreage that surrounded my village. As I gazed out over the fields, I perceived them to be strangely empty except for a few scattered scarecrows.

Quickly, we crested the top of a hill and there, spread out before us, laid the outer walls of Dereham. Swiftly we traveled the last half-mile and arrived at the wall. Stopping at the main gate, we were surprised to find that is was left open with no sentries to guard it. It appeared that none of Cyrus' hired rogues had any loyalty and none had returned to warn him. The fat man had no idea of my whereabouts. He probably presumed that his cutthroats, with the help of Ralph McCracken's treachery, had already taken care of me.

We entered through the gate and I carefully guided our party of men down a side lane. Trying to be as inconspicuous as possible, we trotted quietly toward my parent's manor, the main keep. The streets were mostly empty, but the few people we did pass peered at us suspiciously. I wondered if any of them recognized me. I doubted it, for I was much thinner and more muscular than ever before and my hair had grown long.

Passing the town's cobblestone bakery and seeing my own village for the first time after such a long absence, I began to feel more confident. I turned to Sir Richard and spoke. "Be ready for anything, but let me deal with Cyrus. And don't assist me even if it appears I need help. This is my village and this is my fight."

Sir Richard nodded. "We'll be ready, and Cyrus is yours."

"Good," I replied as we rounded a corner and the inner high walls encircling my home appeared before us.

I should have felt delighted when I saw those thick stone barriers. Instead, my confidence waned knowing that Cyrus stood somewhere back behind those walls. I again felt a staggering bolt of fear. I halted my horse in its tracks and stared blankly ahead. I couldn't go on, I was paralyzed.

Our party of men stopped their beasts and Eric asked, "What is it Winston?"

I didn't answer immediately, for I didn't know what to say. I didn't want to tell him that I couldn't go on. I didn't want to admit that I was afraid and a coward. Then suddenly the sweet face of Meranda shone in my mind and I knew I wouldn't have to confess anything. She was inside those walls too and she needed me. "Nothing," I replied as I spurred my horse up to the entrance of the keep.

This gate too was left open, but it appeared to be guarded at least perfunctorily. A lanky nearly toothless man with a golden beard stepped in front of us defiantly. He apparently didn't notice how large our group of men was.

"And what party may you be?" he asked in a nasally voice. "Have you got your invitations? Wha—Winston?" His eyes opened wide when he realized who I was and he pulled out his sword. Then he glanced to his left and to his right and made a gesturing motion with his hands. Two men, one on each side of him, stepped out from behind the gates displaying swords and shields.

I pulled my blade from its scabbard and glared intensely into the eyes of the nearly toothless man. Calmly I said, "You shall let us pass peacefully by or you shall die."

He stood for a moment, stealing a couple of quick glances at the men on either side of him. Then he stepped back, along with the other two, and made room for us to pass.

"You're a wise man," I said as I rode by.

He nodded his head slightly, but no words came from his lips. I noticed his hands trembling as he placed his sword back into its sheath and the front of his trousers were wet where they had been dry a moment before.

Entering the courtyard, I saw that it was empty except for a few bewildered looking servants coming in and out of the bakery and brew house. Passing the larder and pantry, I galloped over to the stable and dismounted. After handing the reins of my horse to Eric, I bolted toward the chapel.

Flinging the doors open wide, I rushed inside. At the end of the pews, near the pulpit, stood the fat man. Beside him was Meranda and in front of both of them stood Douglas the local priest. Most of the guests attending appeared to be locals from Dereham and instantly all their eyes were upon me. A hush enveloped the room and a twinge of fear again swept over me.

"Winston?" whispered the soft voice of Meranda.

My eyes found hers and we gazed upon each other. She was magnificently dressed in a flowing gown of white. Her long golden hair was pulled up on top of her head and it appeared held together with wild flowers. Her eyes of blue seemed to call out to me for help. All the fears my heart contained were washed away in that instant and I smiled.

Then I gazed upon Cyrus. His pear shaped body, now more plentiful than ever, was covered in a fresh new surcoat displaying the colors of my own family. Luckily, he still held the ring, which he had planned to give Meranda, in his pudgy little hands. Thus, I knew he had not yet shamed her in marriage. A look of disbelief appeared in his small black eyes and beads of sweat quickly formed on his wide forehead. His thick bald skull glistened in the candlelight and his heavy cheeks were flushed.

Cyrus swept his eyes about the room, but when he saw that there was no escape, he began to speak. "There he is!" he shouted, slurring his words. While pointing at me, he eyed the wedding guests. "There's the murdering fiend! He's the one who killed Lord Tabor! Arrest him!"

No one moved a muscle; they just stared in amazement at the scene being played out before them.

"Go on, I command you!" screamed Cyrus, stepping forward and glaring more intensely at the guests in the pews. "As loyal servants to me, Lord Everett, I command you to arrest this scoundrel!"

"Why don't you do it yourself?" I asked.

Appearing drunk, he stumbled forward. "That I will!"

Just then, the doors opened behind me. Eric, Sir David, and a few other knights clambered into the chapel. After nodding at them, I turned back toward Cyrus and spoke. "So, you thought you could kill my father, blame it on me, and become Lord of this manor?"

"That's a lie!" replied Cyrus.

"You even convinced my mother that it was I who killed my father. That was cunning, but did you have to murder her too?"

"That's another lie you drunken bastard!" yelled Cyrus as he pulled out his blade.

"This time, I believe, it's you who are drunk!" I exclaimed while drawing my sword.

The fat man came at me, thrusting his blade with all the force that his voluminous body could produce.

I blocked his thrust and pivoted on my right foot in a circle around him. This brought me directly behind his massive girth and I kicked him in the rear. "Let's take it outside," I said as he tumbled head over heels through the chapel doors.

Eric and the knights roared with laughter, as did many of the guests, at the site of such an enormous man rolling along the ground.

Before following Cyrus outdoors, I turned to Meranda and blew her a kiss. She smiled delicately. Then I stepped out into the courtyard just as Cyrus was standing.

"I should have killed you the first time!" he yelled as he came at me again.

He thrust, I blocked. He swung, I blocked. He jabbed and I blocked again. We went on like this for a few moments while I observed his ability with the blade. I realized that the fear I had held earlier for the man who now stood before me hadn't been based on reason. Cyrus was a competent swordsman in Christendom, but, as Emery had taught me, that meant very little in reality. His only skill was of thrusting, jabbing, and hacking. It was probably his loud demeanor and enormous size that had made me and most other men fear him so.

As I continued to parley with Cyrus, I determined that I was correct in my earlier assumption that he had already had a bit too much to drink on his wedding day. Knowing this, I decided to ask him the same question he had once asked me. "Is it a fool, or a drunk, or the two combined, who lets his own anger get the best of him?"

Cyrus didn't answer. He was tiring and breathing heavily. With each gasp of air he made a snorting sound resembling a pig.

I took my eyes off of the brute for a moment and noticed that everyone who had been in the chapel was now outside, including Meranda. She stood nearby watching and as my eyes gazed upon her, Cyrus swung his blade and nearly cut my chest open. Fortunately, I noticed his motion from the corner of my eye and I leaped out of the way just in time. I began thrusting my sword back at him and, as I had suspected, the fat man's only defense was to retreat.

Halting my attack for a moment, I shouted, "I might let you live if you admit your guilt!"

"It is I who decides who lives or dies!" he gasped.

At that instant I stepped forward and thrust my blade toward his torso. As planned, he swung his sword down to block it. As he did, I quickly pushed my blade down and then spun it up and around in a circular motion and sliced off his right ear. The white piece of flesh fell to the earth and blood began to trickle from the side of Cyrus' head.

The fat man brought his left hand up and around to the wound, pulled it away, and then gazed at his fingers. Crimson dripped from their tips and a look of fright appeared on Cyrus' face. It was a look I hadn't seen before.

"Admit it Cyrus, in front of everyone! Admit the evil you have done to my family! Clear my good name and you might live!"

Cyrus didn't answer; his mouth was too busy sucking air. He backed away from me, but I didn't follow. Instead, I stood still for a moment, letting him rest.

While standing there, and though no one said it aloud, it seemed to me that the crowd of spectators were rooting for me. I had the feeling that most of those who had been invited to the wedding attended only out of fear and not because they held Cyrus in high regard. I also knew that none of them would openly encourage me, for if I were defeated they would face the fat man's wrath.

"Well Cyrus, are you ready to tell the truth?" I asked.

He glared at me like a raging bull, his eyes full of hatred and fear, but he said nothing. The courtyard fell silent except for the loud sound of Cyrus' wheezing. The massive brute appeared exhausted and blood still trickled from his wound, yet I felt no pity for him, only loathing.

"Do you want to tell these people how you chased me out into the forest to kill me?" I asked. "And how once you thought I was dead you murdered your comrade Hector—because he knew the truth about you? Because he knew you had killed my father in cold blood and had blamed it on me?"

"Shut up!" yelled Cyrus.

"As I lay there in the dirt near death, I watched you murder Hector! Like a coward, you stabbed him in the back!"

Cyrus couldn't take it anymore. "Liar!" he screamed and he came at me with his blade.

Again, I let him make his move before I took any action and when he jabbed at me, I blocked his sword with mine. Then, quickly spinning around, I swung my blade into the back of his left ankle and he tumbled to the ground.

"What's wrong Cyrus? Don't you want these people to know what a coward you are?" I gestured with a wave of my hand toward the townsfolk who were watching. As I did, many of them looked away or glanced down at the ground as if pretending not to see the spectacle before them. They were still afraid of Cyrus, even when he was in such a terrible state.

I watched the fat man for a moment as he attempted to stand. He couldn't, for my blade had cut the sinew and muscle in the back of his ankle, which was needed to coordinate his balance.

Suddenly, Cyrus raised himself on his right leg and twisted his body to face me. Desperately, he thrust his sword forward and tried to gore me, but I stepped backward and dodged the blow. I jabbed the point of my blade into his right hand and caught the hilt of his sword. With a flick of my wrist, his weapon went sailing through the air.

As Cyrus' eyes followed his sword, I immediately found myself bringing my blade down upon his other ear. An instant later, the chunk of flesh hit the dirt with a spatter of crimson.

I stood and gazed down at the huge beast of a man before me. He was a sight to behold, kneeling on the ground with his hands placed over the sides of his head. Blood trickled out between the cracks of his fingers, rolled down his face, and dripped onto his surcoat. His thick lips quivered as if to speak, but nothing came from them.

At that moment, I began to feel the sweet pleasure of revenge. Yet before my vengeance was complete, I needed Cyrus to admit his crimes in front of all the townsfolk, so I could clear the good name of Tabor. Knowing that Cyrus was a coward, I lifted my sword high above his head as though I might cut him down at any moment. "Say your prayers!" I said.

"No!" he screamed, placing his crimson covered hands upon my breeches and begging, "let me live! I'll admit it! Just let me live— please!"

My plan had worked. "Go on, say it!" I shouted, lifting my sword even higher to ensure he'd continue with his confession.

"Yes," he bellowed, "I killed Lord Tabor!"

"And my mother?"

"Yes, yes!" he sobbed, placing his head into his hands. "It was I! Just please leave me be!"

"And why should I let a filthy pig like you live? Did you have any mercy for my father and mother, or the old hermit? Did you give them a chance to beg for their lives?"

Cyrus looked up in horror, only now realizing that his admission of guilt had sealed his fate and that I would not forgive him. "No! No! Please!" he cried.

I began to bring my sword down upon him, but as I did, I glanced up for just an instant and saw the innocent eyes of Meranda upon me. I halted my sword in mid-swing, just an inch from the left angle of Cyrus' neck and shoulder. Cyrus screamed out like some strange beast and I looked down at him to see him sobbing uncontrollably. Though I hated him more than anything in the world and I so wanted to drink from the sweet cup of revenge, I couldn't bring myself to kill him in front of Meranda. I jabbed my sword into the ground next to the pitiful man and said, "Take this disgraceful coward to the Dungeon!"

A number of Eric and Lord Stanton's men picked up the wailing Cyrus Everett and led him away. I knew I would eventually obtain my revenge, though it would not be as quick as I had hoped. I was confident that after the county steward was notified, Cyrus would be found guilty. Then he would surely face the executioner.

The crowd cheered as they gathered around me and words of relief and delight rang in my ears. "Thank you Winston! He was an evil man! We knew he was lying, we just couldn't prove it! We knew you'd come back! It's great to have you home!"

I didn't stay to listen. Instead, I found myself groping through the crowd toward Meranda where she stood silently gazing at me. When I reached her I didn't know what to say. Before I could speak, she flung herself into my arms.

"Winston, thank God you returned!" she cried as tears streamed down her tender cheeks. "I'm sorry for doubting you, but it seemed—"

"Shhhh! It's over," I whispered. "We needn't worry about what has happened in the past. I'm just grateful you're safe."

She smiled and wiped away her tears with the sleeve of her gown. Her innocent blue eyes bashfully darted back and forth from the ground to me. "I still love you, you know."

When she said those words, my heart exploded with joy and suddenly I found myself down on one knee. I took her hand. "Will you marry me?"

She blushed and then in her delicate way, she replied, "Yes Lord Tabor, I will."

"Hurray!" cheered the crowd instantly.

I glanced around, having forgotten where I was, and felt a bit embarrassed. It didn't matter though, for I was holding the hand of the girl I truly loved.

Just then, one of my father's lady house servants hastened up to me and spoke. "Excuse me, my lord, but the servants and I were preparing a feast. After all that's happened, we're not sure whether we should continue?"

My eyes quickly found Meranda's and I could tell she knew what I was thinking. She nodded her head and smiled.

"Yes," I said to the servant, "prepare the feast! Today is a joyous day, for we shall be wedded!"

"Hurray!" again yelled the throng of people who surrounded us.

"Break out the ale!" shouted someone in the crowd.

Meranda and I began strolling happily toward the chapel when an old gray terrier ran up to us. His wiry tail was wagging quickly back and forth. "Jiggers!" I exclaimed, kneeling down to stroke his head. "Where did you come from?"

"Down by the stream where we used to meet," replied Meranda. "I thought of you often, so I went to the stream many times hoping that you might still be hiding nearby. I found the old dog there and he followed me home."

"That's wonderful." I said, scratching behind Jigger's ears.

Then I stood and unexpectedly a short bearded man thrust a mug of ale into my hand. "A toast," he said, "to you Winston Tabor, for liberating Dereham from that evil man, Cyrus Everett!"

"Yeah!" roared the crowd.

I raised the mug of ale to my lips, surmising that if there was ever a time to celebrate with drink it was now. I tipped the container and felt the warm liquid spill into my mouth and douse my tongue. Suddenly, the words that Emery had once told me echoed in my mind. 'You can't even have one sip, or all you have gained will be lost. You must always remember that you're happier now than when the ale controlled your soul.' Yes, that was the truth and I believed it! I spit out the ale before it had entered my throat and threw down the mug.

"Water!" I shouted. "I toast only with water!"

The crowd became quiet and all eyes fell upon me. The people of Dereham remembered me only as a drunkard, a shameful son to my father, but there I was before them refusing drink.

"Here you go my lord."

I turned to see who had spoken. It was the same lady servant who had questioned me about the feast.

"Tis safe to drink," she said, handing me a wooden cup, "it comes from deep in the well."

"Alright then," Eric spoke up, "how about that toast? To Winston, Lord of Dereham!"

The crowd repeated the toast and followed it with a resounding cheer. Then, as everyone tipped back their mugs, I lifted the cool cup of water to my lips and drank heartily.

Next, I took Meranda into my arms and tenderly kissed her. It was the most jubilant day I had ever known. Still, my smile grew just a bit wider when, through all the cheer and merriment, I heard the familiar voice of Donovan yell out, "To Winston, the Drinkwater!"